THUNDER

Barbara Winkes

There's rain inside
my mind and thunder
rattles me every time
I think of you

-Lauren Eve, *A Fractured & Luminous Soul*

For D.

Chapter One

Kelli Jameson

I hate everything about this case. Even only a few miles from my destination, I can hardly understand how I got here, the task at hand becoming more daunting with every minute. There's a reason and a story. There always is. When did I miss the point of no return?

The city has long given way to suburban, and now, rural areas. Out here, I drive through smaller towns and farmland. For long stretches there's nothing but earth and sky, not enough distractions.

The only saving grace is that I won't have to stay long in this place. Claustrophobic, agoraphobic, I'm not even sure anymore, but the unfamiliar setting is getting to me. Perhaps it has to do with my expectations.

Redeem myself and find out what happened to a missing teen, report back to my boss, get on with life.

The problem is I'm not much interested in finding out what happened to Lucas Gavin who, at seventeen, raped a girl at a party. He's eighteen now, went to trial and got off with nothing more than a slap on the wrist, if you can even call it that. A predictable story: Like Lucas's father, the judge, prosecutor, and defense attorney were all affluent white men—privilege in

1

action. Everyone was hesitant to interfere with Lucas's shining bright future, because of that one "mistake." From the transcripts I've read, no one seemed to give much of a damn about the girl's future.

It's a mountain of problems, with this town, with society at large, but I have one clearly defined job: Find Lucas, who went missing five days ago.

I all but begged my boss to send someone else, but he knew I couldn't say no. He also went to college with Lucas Gavin's parents and wants to do them a favor.

Here I am, miserable and angry at the world, though I'm aware my feelings are irrelevant compared to what Erica McQuade and her family have gone through.

I wish I could do something for them.

I arrive in town around four-fifty. Having skipped lunch earlier, I consider an early dinner, but the sooner I get to work, the sooner I can leave again.

At the inn, a bored employee provides me with a key and informs me that they lock the doors at ten. Whatever. I don't plan on staying out to party, not that there would be any place for it. After freshening up in the modest room, I take another look at my map and the list of people to see.

The Gavins.

The McQuades.

With a little luck, I'll have a lead, and that little shit will be home with his parents soon. I imagine that even though he won in court, people on social media aren't silent. He's probably hiding out and drinking somewhere…Best case scenario would be to catch him committing a crime, so he could be held accountable this time. Even better if that happens in a place where his parents don't feel like they have "jurisdiction."

I shake myself out of the fantasy and go back down to my car. Lucas's parents reported him missing to the local police. I drove past the small station earlier. They're probably understaffed.

I want to know if Mr. and Mrs. Gavin left out parts of the story. I'm quite a bit out of my jurisdiction too, but that doesn't mean I can't judge any of them, for covering up a crime and being self-righteous about it.

The Gavins' house is one of the biggest in town, brightly white, balconies and pillars. I feel sick already, but that could be from the hot humid weather or lack of food. I hope that later I can find a place where I can have a decent meal and a beer. There's no way I can survive these days completely sober, not with what happened in mind.

Predictably, it's an employee who opens the front door to me. I'll admit I came with a ton of preconceived notions about this family. If the son thought that he could get away with rape—and he did—what do the parents have to hide? Did they lock the housekeeper's passport in a safe and force her to work around the clock? Nothing about what some people do to others surprises me anymore. Greed and entitlement explain so much.

"I'm Kelli Jameson," I say when the silence turns awkward. "Mr. and Mrs. Gavin expect me."

"Yes. Please come with me."

Inside the Gavins' home, the luxury is surprisingly understated, but still noticeable. The grand entrance, the stairs, the furnishing...There's a lot of money here. The woman leads me to a den where the two occupants of the room jump to their feet. I notice the whiskey on the table.

"Ms. Jameson. We're so glad you could make it."

Like I had a choice. I choke back the retort and fake a smile as I shake Mr. Gavin's hand.

"Mr. and Mrs. Gavin. I'll do what I can to help find Lucas."

"That's good, because the police aren't doing a damn thing."

Mrs. Gavin flinches but doesn't comment. Her gaze is haunted, though if it's from worry for her son, or because of what he did—it's too early to tell.

"Please, sit," she says, her voice soft. "Can I offer you anything?"

"No, thank you." The sooner I can leave the better. "I just need to ask you a few questions."

"Of course," Mr. Gavin acknowledges. "I assume you read our statements. There's nothing much to add to that, I'm afraid. We're worried. Lucas was acquitted, but those rabid people on the Internet just wouldn't let it go."

"Are you aware of any specific threats?"

I'm sure Erica had to deal with all of it and worse, though the Gavins don't seem to be concerned about her.

"Just the usual garbage," he said, sounding disgusted. "The world has gone crazy, right? Lucas showed bad judgment one time, and they want to burn him at the stake. They were drunk teenagers messing around, but they think he should be the only one to pay."

"Well, he was the one accused of the crime. Maybe some felt there wasn't enough accountability."

The words are out of my mouth before I can hear my boss's warning words in my head. Damn, it's happening early.

"Accountability? Our family's name was dragged through the mud. At least, in the end some reasonable people put an end to that. I didn't think it was your job to rehash all that."

"No, sir, I'm sorry," I say through gritted teeth. I have to be more careful if I don't want them to call my boss the moment I leave their house. "It's true, I read your statements. In my experience, there is a lot that teenagers won't tell their parents—but they'll tell their friends. Kyle Vance was a witness in the trial, and he mentioned a Pete...Bradley. Do you know if they kept in touch?"

"I think Pete went back to school, but he visits his parents regularly. Kyle came back to support Lucas. They've been friends for a long time. What are you insinuating?"

"Nothing. They might be aware of specific threats online or otherwise, but I'll check with them. You said Pete went back...Lucas and Kyle didn't?"

"What do you think? The school had to take him back, because he did nothing wrong, but there were protesters making his life hell. He was taking a break, staying here for a while, and looking at his options."

Cry me a river. I almost said that out loud.

"Do you know if he contacted Erica McQuade after the trial?"

"What the hell is that supposed to mean? After those wild accusations? I think he has had enough of her."

I ignore his grandstanding, thinking there's a myriad of possibilities, none of them good. My primary theory is still that I could find Lucas in a motel room somewhere, with his buddies, drinking and getting high. Feeling sorry for themselves.

If he came back here and tried to threaten Erica, someone might have taken offense. Erica, her parents, someone who decided enough is enough...I don't want to get tangled up in any of this.

"I'll talk to Kyle and Pete," I say. "Is there anyone else who might know where Lucas went? His girlfriend?"

"He doesn't have a girlfriend," Mrs. Gavin replies. "He was focusing on his studies."

That, and partying, but I don't say it out loud. If I offend them any more on my first visit, I might be out of a job soon, and as much as I hate it right now, it still pays the bills.

I was right about them though. They're the kind of family who would be found in church every Sunday, front row, to make sure they'd be seen. They rage about how unfair it is, but the truth is, being at the center of this story plays into their ideas of martyrdom.

"Okay. If you remember anything else, please don't hesitate to call me. You can reach me on my cell." I hand one of the business cards I had printed yesterday, to Gavin. "I'm sure we'll find Lucas soon."

I'm not sure why, but I feel the need to add this. Perhaps under all this entitlement, they're parents, scared for their child. I wonder how far that fear can go to help them ignore the grave reality of his behavior...and that he might be doing it again as we speak.

One "mistake." Or a predator in the making.

꧁꧂

From the Gavins' I go straight to another set of angry, grieving parents, though this time, I can sympathize. I don't want to be here either, add to their grief, but there's the possibility that someone in this house can help me find out what happened. I hope it will be just this one visit, to rule them out and leave them in peace after this.

Mr. McQuade, Erica's father, doesn't seem ready to believe me.

"You're working for those people, no, I don't want you in my house."

"Please, Mr. McQuade, I'm not trying to deny what Lucas did. I'm sorry. Mr. and Mrs. Gavin only hired me to find their son."

He scoffs. "It's better for anyone if the bastard stays in whatever hole he's hiding in."

I can't say I disagree.

"Could I please come in for a minute? I swear, I'm not trying to make things harder for your family. If I could have one moment with Erica?"

He stares at me, unimpressed. "I don't know you. Why the hell should we trust you?"

"Because I know Erica told the truth. I believe her. But if this drags on longer, people might start pointing fingers, and Lucas Gavin becomes some sort of martyr in the story. The sooner I can find him, the sooner things can go back to normal."

And I can go home, though that is in no way relevant to him and his daughter.

"Normal?" He laughs bitterly, but steps aside to let me inside. Two steps into the house, I can already see how money and odds were stacked against the family in the trial. I don't mind his anger. I share it.

"Bad choice of words. I'm sorry. I know you've been through hell. If I could ask Erica a couple of questions? I don't mind if you're present. I have nothing to hide."

"Neither have I." Erica McQuade comes down the stairs, her dark eyes big in her pale face. Her tone is quiet and determined though. "I can talk to you."

"That's great. Thank you so much."

"Erica, you don't have to do that."

"It's okay, Dad."

"Please, you have nothing to worry about," I try to assure them both. "This will only take a few minutes."

Erica squares her shoulders.

"Come on up."

Her father looks like he wants to protest, but he remains standing in the middle of the room, exuding an air of anger and helplessness. I can't blame him.

Upstairs, Erica leads me to her room. I swallow hard at the sight of the teddy bear on one of the shelves. She's sixteen. I curse my boss, and his besties who spawned evil like Lucas. A mistake, my ass.

He should be in jail.

"I agree, but that ship has sailed, hasn't it?" Erica's sarcastic response alerts me to the fact that I'll have to work harder to keep my thoughts to myself. I actually said this out loud.

"I don't want to make this any harder for you or your family. All I have to know is if Lucas has contacted you recently. Maybe in a text message?"

She shakes her head.

"If he did, that's not your fault, and it's not all right. He will be—"

"What, held accountable?"

I don't blame her for her skepticism. I wouldn't believe it if I was her.

"Would you allow me to take a look at your phone?"

"Why?" There's a hint of suspicion to her tone, but then she continues, "You'd like to see all the messages from his friends calling me a liar and a whore? It's nothing new or surprising, I can tell you."

"I'm so sorry. No one should have to go through this. Has anyone threatened you?"

She shrugs, her attempt at nonchalance not all that convincing. "I think his lawyer told Lucas not to contact me. As for the others..." Erica lets her words trail off, her eyes glistening with tears. I hate myself a little more, for being naïve enough to think I could do this without dragging her and her parents back to that place.

"Have you gotten any help?"

"I see a therapist out of town. It's going okay," she says, though she doesn't sound much convinced. "Eventually, people will move on and stop talking."

That might be wishful thinking. I've seen this town. The case gave the people a lot to talk about and cement their prejudice about girls tempting boys with a promising future. How does anyone live around here without wanting to drink all day?

"Maybe. I wish you all the best, Erica. If you think of anything that might help me, or if you need to talk, please call me."

"Why would I want to talk to you?" Now, there's an understandable hint of irritation to her tone.

"That's a good question," I admit. "I'll leave you alone, but I hope you can talk to your friends."

What is wrong with me? Stay in my lane, ask the questions, get out. That's the job.

"My so-called friends bailed on me," she says, and for the first time, anger breaks through her quiet, reserved demeanor.

"That sucks. They sided with Lucas?"

"They just stopped coming around. I guess I know now that I could never rely on them."

"That's right." Mr. McQuade is standing in the doorway, alerting me to the fact that the interview is over. "Those girls showed their true colors when they failed to stand up for Erica."

"Dad, she doesn't want to know about that."

"Doesn't matter. Mom will be here in a bit. Ms. Jameson?"

"Yes, we're done here. Thank you both so much for talking to me."

I follow him back down the stairs while Erica stays in her room.

"Those girls, can you tell me their names?" I ask.

"Why? What good would that do? You think they know where the weasel went?" He shakes his head, relenting. "Fiona Collins, Lexi Adams and Amanda Rutherford. They used to come around all the time, but from the moment it happened…nothing. You get to know somebody when you really need them, don't you?"

"I guess so. Thanks again, Mr. McQuade."

I extend my hand, and he shakes it reluctantly, still cautious. He sees me to the door and closes it behind me as I walk down the steps of the porch and to my car. Before I get inside, I look up and see movement behind an upstairs window. Erica's room. I wonder if she has something else to tell me, but it won't happen right now.

I sit behind the wheel and jot down the names Mr. McQuade gave me, thinking this is getting worse by the minute. I have to interview a bunch of conspiring and drama-prone teens now. It's nothing compared to what Erica went through, but I'm not looking forward to it either.

Chapter Two

I n my hotel room, I add to my notes and come up with a plan for the next day. I can't make Erica give up her phone, but perhaps Kyle Vance is worried enough about his pal to talk to me. I'm not sure what's worse, Lucas's friends standing by him and possibly lying for him in court, or Erica's friends refusing to stand up for her.

Meanwhile, as I explore the town in search of a place to have dinner, I notice the looks. People around here recognize a newcomer, as it seems, though they are more curious than hostile. Word gets around, and they probably know it's the Gavins who hired me. The ones with the son whose bright future was barely touched.

Right, this is not helping. I need to take a step back to be able to do my job. Unlike other people in this town, I'm not trapped by stereotypes and geography. Once my job is done, for better or worse, I'll go home to the city and all its comforts.

I can't wait.

For the moment, I'll be happy with a burger and a cold beer.

I come to a place that probably accounts for a main street, with some shops, a café, and a restaurant. As I look around, I don't see many alternatives, so I step inside the latter. It's more of a bar, but not too rundown. I go straight to the counter and order their menu of the day, a cheeseburger with fries, and a pint. Why start small? I'll walk back to my hotel room. If anyone wants to judge me, I don't care.

To my relief, the people in here don't seem to pay much attention to me. I see a woman and a man having dinner, local cops, I guess from overhearing snippets of their conversation. One family with older children. I catch the curious look of the teenage girl and wonder if I should convey a message to her. *Run while you can.* She averts her gaze and smiles at her younger brother.

My food arrives, and I dig in, barely suppressing a sigh of relief after the first sip of beer. It's good indeed, and after this day, I feel like I deserve it. There's air-conditioning, and for a few brief moments, all is good with the world.

Even in this Godforsaken town.

Now, if I said that out loud, they might throw me out, so I content myself with enjoying my meal.

Like I said before, there's nothing much to distract me from the disastrous matter at hand. As I survey the patrons coming and going, I wonder whose side they have taken, and how some of them sleep at night. Or maybe they don't, lying awake fearing that one day, their daughter could be vilified on the Internet and in court, being called a liar and a whore.

Will we never get beyond that?

As long as people like the Gavins are still calling the shots in small towns like this, I guess there's not much hope. Or maybe I just have a special hate for certain small towns, because nothing good seems to ever happen in them.

Lucas and his buddies were home for the summer. Erica might have planned to leave for college, but now she is hiding out at her parents'. Lucas Gavin was looking at his "options," and his friends were likely to still harass his victim.

If karma is a real thing, it needs to come back to all those young men—and my boss, for sending me into this nightmare.

I have a phone number for Pete Bradley, but I only reach his voicemail and leave a message.

I'm Kelli Jameson, the PI Mr. and Mrs. Gavin hired to find Lucas. I was hoping we could talk. Please call me back any time.

I don't have much hope that he'll respond to that, but I'll try again until I reach him. Something tells me that the three of them shared more secrets than I'm able to guess at the moment.

The hotel room comes with a surprisingly generous breakfast buffet, and I'm taking advantage, knowing it will be another long, tedious day. On top of it all, I'm in another time zone. There's only one other guest sitting at a table in the corner, a man in a suit talking on the phone. An employee refills my coffee cup from time to time.

The town doesn't seem to have much to offer in terms of tourism—another reason why strangers stand out. Not my problem. Next on my list is Kyle Vance who swore on the stand that Erica consented to having sex with Lucas.

There's still the chance that this could be over soon. Vance, Lucas's best buddy, is living by himself in an apartment in a more suburban area. Perhaps he's hiding him? One phone call, and I could go home?

Part of me has already resigned to the fact that it would be too easy. People like Lucas and Kyle aren't the types to retreat. Gloating is more their thing, and from what I could tell, they did plenty of that.

Their social media accounts are locked. Neither of them ever wavered from stating that Lucas did nothing wrong. According to them, Erica was worried about her reputation the next day, having regrets, and that's why she went to the police. They stuck to that story from the first statement to the press release, and throughout the trial.

It's true—Lucas's disappearance is curious. I'm not sure that I want to know what's behind it.

Kyle is home, and he agrees to see me. It's about a half hour drive. He's nineteen and in college. I know the moment I walk inside the place that he's not paying for it, unless he got an advance on his inheritance, trust fund or both.

"Hey. You're the PI," he says. "Come on in."

He's comfortable. There's not a hint of worry or shame. When they said Lucas did nothing wrong, it's not just because they want to disguise the truth. It's that they believe this *is* the truth, that Erica's word isn't worth as much. The breakfast I enjoyed earlier sits heavy in my stomach.

"Lucas's parents told me you're his best friend. You must be worried."

"Should I be? Did you find out anything new?"

"I was hoping you could help me. When was the last time you talked to him?"

He shrugs, as if unsure about the answer. "A week ago maybe?"

"Maybe?"

"Okay, a week ago. I told that to the police already, but I understand why his parents hired someone. They're not doing all that much. I wonder if someone should talk to the higher-ups."

"You think they're not doing their jobs?"

"It sure looks that way," he claims. "Perhaps they bought into the lies some people have been telling about Lucas."

"You told the truth, though." I did a decent job hiding the sarcasm, but he still catches up on the fact that I'm not all that sympathetic.

"Of course, I did. What is this about? I thought you wanted to find Lucas."

That hint of anger when they don't get their will immediately. I saw it with Mr. Gavin too.

"That's the plan. So, when you talked to him, did he seem okay? Was he worried about anything?"

He sits down on what must be an expensive leather couch but doesn't offer me a seat.

"We talked on the phone. Nothing out of the ordinary. He talked about a couple of schools he wanted to visit."

Options.

"You're not going back to college?"

"After what that bitch did? No, I'm taking a year off, helping my parents with their business."

If it wasn't for the stupid, predictable slur, I would have laughed. He wasn't helping anyone, just hanging out in his luxury apartment in the middle of the day.

Affluenza Central. I went to school with boys like that. Back in the day, we didn't see much of a choice but to stay far away and warn others to do the same. Has anything really changed that much?

"Okay then. Before that last call, is there anything you can remember…Someone being mad at Lucas, or threatening him?"

"No," he says a little too quickly.

"You're still sending threatening messages to Erica. That didn't make anyone angry?"

"She told you that?" he asks with an air of contempt. "No surprise there. She's lying again."

"Just out of curiosity, if you think she made everything up—"

"Which she did. You know my statement."

"Why would she do anything like that? What's in it for her?"

"Who knows? Maybe she thought she could get money out of Lucas. That obviously backfired. You shouldn't be asking these questions. The trial is over. The truth came out."

I have to wrap this up. There's no way I can pretend much longer that I don't want to punch his smug face.

"If Lucas contacts you, let me know. It's important. His parents are worried, and maybe you should be too."

His eyes narrow. "What the hell are you talking about? They hired you to find him, and you're threatening me?"

"I'm not threatening you, Kyle, just stating the facts. If he's cooling his heels somewhere, fine, but there are other possibilities. Not everyone was happy with the outcome of the trial, I imagine. They might think both you and Lucas lied on the stand."

"That's ridiculous," he scoffs. "We told the truth. Lucas is probably hanging with a friend."

"What friend? Pete? Or could you give me any other name?"

"Yeah, maybe check with Pete, I don't know anyone else he could be with. Is that all?"

"Sure. Thanks for your time, Mr. Vance."

At least, in the next phase of my inquiries, I don't have to deal with raw grief or unveiled bigotry which is a plus...Not by that much, because now I have to go to high school and talk to the mean girls. Everything about this feels wrong, but that's summing up the whole story.

I have a feeling. The fact that those girls let Erica down this harshly might be unrelated to Lucas's disappearance. My instincts tell me otherwise. Lucas's mother told me he didn't have a girlfriend—given his good-boy, promising-athlete image, I have trouble believing that. And if someone from Erica's group of friends was the one, his actions and lies might have poisoned those friendships beyond repair.

The high school's campus is small, and I have no trouble finding Ms. Burke's history class. I lurk in the doorway until I recognize two of the girls from their social media profiles.

"Amanda and Lexi?"

They both turn to me with a look of suspicion.

"Who wants to know?" Lexi asks.

"I'm Kelli Jameson, a private investigator. Could I ask you a few questions?"

"About what?"

"Lucas Gavin. You heard that he disappeared?"

Lexi keeps giving me a hard stare while Amanda shrugs. "People are talking. He got a lot of attention online, maybe he needed a break."

Really? *He* needed a break? I don't even know what to make of that. All I know is I'm angry, and there's not enough alcohol in the world to get me to a place where I'll ever be all right again. If my boss wanted to teach me a lesson, I'm not sure what it is.

If I don't lose my job over this, I might quit myself.

"His parents are worried about him. You guys don't happen to know where he might be taking that break?"

The two girls share a quick look.

"Why would we? We're not friends with him. He wouldn't tell either of us."

"About that. You were friends with Erica, right? What happened there?"

"I thought this was about Lucas," Lexi says. "But if you must know, too much drama."

"Drama? He raped her!"

I'm seriously close to shaking her.

"Is everything all right?"

We all turn into the direction of that voice, a surprising amount of authority coming from the woman several inches smaller than me. Wavy auburn hair falls past her shoulders. She's

17

probably in her thirties, though her more conservative choice of clothing, with the twin set and dark skirt, is misleading.

"We have to go," Amanda says, and she and Lexi walk inside the room.

"Ms. Merin Burke, I assume."

"Yes. And you are?" She's suspicious too.

I introduce myself to her and explain my presence. "I was wondering if any of your students could help me find Lucas Gavin. His parents can't reach him."

"I'm sorry. I can't help you. I have a class to teach. Good luck finding him."

She all but closes the door in my face.

Chapter Three

I'm happy to leave the grounds of the school for the moment, but I'm not done yet. I find myself a small café where I sit with a coffee and some sort of strawberry pastry I couldn't resist. It's too early to drink, so sugar and caffeine will have to do.

It's frustrating how everyone wants to brush me off, no matter whose side they're on. What people in this town seem to want most is to sweep under the carpet what happened, uncomfortable with frank conversations, unwilling to face reality. Though, this kind of behavior is sadly not limited to this place.

To be honest, I had hoped that by this time, I'd have more of a lead, and an idea when I could go home. There's an immense amount of stonewalling around the subject, though I believe Erica and her dad. They seem to be trying to go the conventional route, therapy, give her time to work through the trauma. I don't see the potential for vigilante justice.

If Lucas isn't partying somewhere…Who besides Erica and her family could be so angry with him that they might have taken measures? Holding him somewhere, or, perhaps, something more extreme? I don't want to open that can of worms. That would mean Erica wasn't the first time.

Come to think of it, that's not unrealistic. Predators never stop with one victim, and many of them start early. I remember seeing the police officers at the bar the other night. I don't think it will do much, but I'll talk to them too, see if they have made any progress.

What if Lucas had a history?

Who would tell me?

I finish my coffee and sweet treat and head back to the school where I lurk in the hallway until Ms. Burke's class is finished. As the students file out one by one, Lexi and Amanda give me another one of those suspicious glances. I'm not at all convinced they told me the whole truth, but I'm not here for them now. After the last student has left, I walk into the room where Ms. Burke is putting papers into her bag.

Looking up, she says, "It's you again."

"Yes, me again."

Did I see the hint of a smile?

"I have to tell you, nothing has changed since the last time I saw you. I still don't know where Lucas is."

I walk closer to her and perch on the edge of her desk.

"I understand that. I was hoping we could talk anyway."

She's a tad annoyed, but not alarmed. "About what?"

"You teach these kids. Erica was in your class as well?"

Mixed emotions are chasing one another in her expression.

"She used to be, yes. The gossiping and the threats, it got too much for her. Honestly, it was too much for everyone. We couldn't protect her." Her regret is palpable.

True, I arrived after most of it was over, but I still have a hard time understanding how everyone in this town could have failed Erica so badly.

"Why not? Because of the Gavins' money?"

She shakes her head with a bitter laugh.

"You're not from around here, Ms. Jameson." She's not asking.

"You haven't answered my question."

"There was an investigation, and a trial, and they found Lucas not guilty."

"You believe that?"

"I have no power whatsoever to change the verdict, neither has Erica, or any of those girls in my class. I'm pretty sure none of them knows where Lucas is, but I can tell you this: If he never comes back, none of us would be sad."

I sense that she, too, harbors a lot of anger and frustration. She's cautious, but there's something genuine about her.

"That's understandable. I'm curious...Erica and her father told me that her friends stopped coming around. Is it because one of them was dating Lucas? So they took his side?"

"No!" The denial is swift, and now she does sound alarmed. "Those girls didn't know what to do with the whole situation. No, it's not fair to Erica, but if they distanced themselves, I don't think it's because they believed Lucas Gavin. It's because they're afraid the same thing could happen to them."

I'm even more grateful that soon enough, I'll be able to leave. I wish the same thing were true for people like her.

"It's a reasonable fear to have, but that kind of behavior won't help them."

My frustration isn't directed at her, or scared teenagers. Maybe Ms. Burke understands that, but either way, she is not interested in prolonging this conversation.

"Maybe. If you'll excuse me now?"

"Sure. Thank you for your time, Ms. Burke."

She gives me a half-hearted shrug as if to say I didn't leave her much of a choice. I watch her walk away, wondering what she's afraid of.

I'll have to ask the Gavins some harder questions.

I'm stalling on the inevitable, because there's a good chance that they will fire me before I'm through with them. Maybe that's a reasonable assumption since I'm about to accuse their son of being a serial predator, but there are only so many explanations left. He already raped someone. People like that don't magically accept that it's wrong—if they got away with it once, they'll try again. And the local court gave him what can only be described as a big fat stamp of approval.

Most of my potential witnesses have proven to be next to useless.

Or am I not seeing what's right in front of me?

I knew this would be bad, but so far, my time here has exceeded my worst expectations—it's a clusterfuck of nepotism and fear. Add to that the oppressive heat hitting me every time I'm not in an air-conditioned building. At least there's a storm in the weather forecast, which might help with that particular aspect.

I have an idea how to reward myself after seeing the Gavins. When I drove out to Kyle Vance's place, I passed by a bar sporting a small rainbow flag on the door. It will be worth making the drive. I need to clear my head. That will work.

I haven't yet talked to Fiona Collins, the third girl Erica used to hang out with. I figure I can do all of it before heading out of town and kicking back a few in a less hostile place.

❧

"Do you know anything?" Mr. Gavin asks in lieu of a greeting. This time, he's the one who opens the door to me before he leads me to the living area. He and his wife look excited. I notice another drink on the table.

"I don't know where Lucas is, I'm sorry. But I have a few more questions."

With mixed feelings, I watch them deflate. Yes, they are parents worried about their child. They are also affluent parents who kept their *criminal* child from being held accountable.

"We told you everything already," he says, not trying to hide his irritation. "What else do you need to know?"

"First of all, did Erica or anyone in her family ever threaten you or Lucas?"

"This is ridiculous. You know she dragged my son into court for nothing!" he tries to deflect.

"Did they?"

"Not that I know of. They kept to themselves. I'm sure the lawyer told them to do that."

"And Lucas didn't contact Erica?"

"No! He was advised not to. Why are you asking these questions?"

"You don't seem to think that he could be in danger from the McQuades. I agree. But if he didn't leave on his own, someone else might be responsible, someone who might be angry at him. It's important that you tell me the truth. Has Lucas ever been in trouble with the law before?"

A few seconds of explosive silence tick by. I brace myself.

"Are you out of your mind?" Mr. Gavin rages. "I'm beginning to think this was a huge mistake. You're supposed to find Lucas, not crucify him for whatever you think it is he did. Our son could be in danger!"

Mrs. Gavin looks aghast. I wonder if it's because of the blasphemy, what might be happening to Lucas, or something they have kept from me.

"Yes, and I'm trying to find him before something grave happens to him. I need you to be honest. Before or after Erica McQuade, were there any other accusations? Could you think of someone who might have taken justice into their own hands?"

"You're out of line, Ms. Jameson," he seethes. "Find my son. If you can't do that, get the hell out of town."

"He never meant to hurt anyone," Mrs. Gavin says, close to tears. Her husband shoots her an angry look as if she already said too much.

"Fine. I'll keep you updated," I tell them. "I can show myself out."

◦◦◦◦

I drive out to Fiona Collins' home next.

"You are Ms. Jameson," Mrs. Collins greets me on her doorstep. News travel at the speed of light in this town. Farmland stretches behind their ranch. I can see the storm clouds in the distance. It's a strange feeling here, as if the sky is going to fall at some point. Maybe it will, swallow up all that hypocrisy—and all of us with it.

Not yet, though.

"Yes. Is Fiona here?"

"She's over at my sister's, the yellow house at the end of the road. You can't miss it."

"Thank you."

I still haven't processed the Gavins' reactions. It's like every possible lead becomes a dead end because no one's telling me the damn truth. I'm not sure I'll actually lose my job if I can't figure out what happened to Lucas. I don't want to take the risk. Also, I'm starting to get pissed at the evasions and smokescreens people put in my way.

A few minutes later, I knock on the door of the two-story house, and a teenage girl opens the door to me.

"Who is it?" a voice from inside calls. A familiar voice. This is getting curious.

"You're Fiona?"

She looks me up and down.

"Yeah. And you're the PI. Amanda called me earlier. She said you were asking questions about Lucas."

"That's true. I'd like to—"

"Fiona!"

"Yes, I'm coming!" She turns and walks to the kitchen. I close the door and follow her.

"We meet again," I say to Merin Burke, the high school teacher. From the looks of it, she's preparing dinner. Standing at the stove, she's now wearing a different skirt and a t-shirt, her hair in a ponytail. She looks a lot younger than in her earlier outfit, her clothes a better fit for her body. I shouldn't even be noticing it, but I do. Maybe because I need something beautiful among all the ugliness, and Merin sure is. Beautiful. And genuine. Everything that seems so rare to come by in this town.

"Yes. You don't seem to be making much headway since you keep coming back to me."

"Actually, your sister told me I could find Fiona here."

"Fiona has nothing to add," Merin states, making it clear that I won't be asking any more questions.

"That's true," Fiona echoes her words. "The girls already told you everything. We don't know where Lucas is."

"I'm sorry you had to come out here for that."

"Don't worry. It's not like I have anything better to do. You have a lovely home."

Merin Burke gives me an amused glance. I have to admit, my attempt at small-town small talk seems a bit of a non-sequitur.

"Thank you," she says. "Fiona, would you mind setting the table? You're still staying?"

"Sure. Are you?" Fiona asks me.

"I don't think so. Whatever your aunt is making smells delicious, but I'm sure she wasn't going to invite me."

With a shrug, Fiona leaves. Turning to her aunt, I realize that she's been studying me.

"You know, you're so curious about all of us, but we don't really know anything about you. Perhaps I should invite you to dinner. I certainly made enough."

"Oh no, I can't impose." The question springs to mind if she lives here alone. I can't detect any hint of children. "But if you want to know anything about me, this is the gist of it. I really hate my job right now. My boss is friends with the Gavins, so he sent me to figure out what happened to Lucas as a favor to them. I believe Erica. I believe what happened is a travesty of justice. Oh, and you can call me Kelli."

"I'm Merin. And perhaps we should talk some more," she says, her tone softening. "I'm sorry I snapped at you earlier, but this has been a rough time for many people. Erica and her family most of all. The Gavins have lots of connections."

"So I've figured, if they could pull strings beyond state lines."

"Yeah. Please stay. George will be home soon, but he'll have to go back to work after dinner. I can't help you solve your case, but I can offer some good pie and coffee."

My trip to the bar with the rainbow flag will have to wait. That might not be such a bad thing, given what I could learn from Merin.

George. That meant she isn't living alone. For a brief, inexplicable moment, I feel disappointed about that revelation. What was I thinking?

Chapter Four

George Burke works as a football coach at the same school as Merin. Judging from his age, I conclude that they were probably high school sweethearts, married early, stayed in the same town where they'd grown up.

What a domestic nightmare, I think. It's none of my business. He's a lot more friendly and polite than most of the people I've met in town, I have to give him that.

"It's a shame what happened," he says. "I try to teach my boys to be responsible, decent human beings. Obviously, Gavin comes from a different culture."

I notice that Fiona is looking down at her plate.

"George," Merin admonishes softly. "We have guests."

"Well, one of our guests is trying to find Gavin, right?" he argues. "That kid is bad news. It wouldn't surprise me if he got himself into more trouble."

"It seems to me that his first call would be to his parents who would then call their lawyer," I say. "But they haven't heard from him."

"I'm sorry we're not of much help. No one's missing him much, to be honest."

"Yeah, I got that impression. People come down on different sides of the story, but no one likes drama much," I say.

Fiona flinches. I assume her friends gave her a play by play of our conversation.

"People have a lot on their plates," he says, his tone still polite and neutral, while Merin all but jumps to her feet.

"Who's ready for dessert?"

George gets up as well. "I'm sorry, but I have to go."

"Me too," Fiona says quickly.

"You want me to give you a ride?"

"Come on. I live down the road."

"It's on the way." Merin's tone leaves little room for an argument. "Too bad for the both of you, Kelli gets to have the strawberry pie first."

<hr />

Dusk hasn't reduced the temperature noticeably. Still, when we sit outside on the porch with coffee and pie, I feel like I'm taking the first deep breath since I arrived here. We can see lightning and hear the faint sound of thunder in the distance. Strong coffee, sweet pie with whipped cream, and pleasant company.

Merin, aunt to one of the terrible three, wife to George.

I have a lot on my mind, and not all of it has to do with the case and how much I hate it.

"That's a nice view you have," I say. My view is pretty nice too.

"Yeah."

"I'm really thankful you invited me into your home. I needed someone to talk to...Half of the town thinks I'm okay because I work for the Gavins, the other half hates me for it. Honestly? I hate myself for it, but I didn't have a choice."

"Everyone has to make hard choices," she says. "I'm not judging anyone else's."

"I think they might have covered up his crimes before. I'm sure they're not telling me everything...not that anyone does around here."

"You think something happened to Lucas, that he's—"

"Dead?" I finish her sentence. "It's a possibility. I just hope this won't lead to more trauma for Erica, and at the same time, I fear it's unavoidable."

"I've known her family for years," Merin says as she stirs milk into her coffee. "They wouldn't—if you think he did something else, maybe it was in his school. Maybe this has nothing to do with the town."

"But he went missing from here," I remind her. "It's bizarre. People tell me he wanted to take a break. He doesn't seem like the type. I think he'd still be gloating about winning the trial."

"Probably," she agrees. "What about you? What are you going to do once you go home?"

"Chase after more low-lives?" I suggest. "I'm not sure. Maybe it's time for a change."

She leans back in her seat. I'm struck by the raw longing in her expression as she looks out at the darkening skyline.

"Change is overrated," she says. "There's comfort in the familiar."

"Or is it the illusion of comfort?"

I jump a bit at the sound when she sets her cup down on the table. I might have struck a nerve.

"Look, I didn't mean to be nosy—"

I have an idea. A nice family home, a straight couple that has been married for some time—no children. Maybe it was their choice, maybe it wasn't.

"It's fine," she says. "Let's finish the coffee. It's going to rain soon."

"Yeah. Again, thank you so much for having me."

She gives me a look I can't interpret, or perhaps it's safer not to try.

"It was my pleasure."

Chapter Five

Merin Burke

By the time George comes home, I have cleared the dishes off the table and sat down with another coffee. Might as well—I haven't slept much lately. Maybe it's the weather that's making me antsy, the storm about to come. Here, we know how to prepare, but that doesn't mean it can't get bad.

"Hey." George pours himself a cup as well and sits. "We still have pie?"

"Sure. In the fridge."

"That was an interesting visit," he says after serving himself. "I'm surprised the Gavins hired someone from out of town."

"You heard what she said earlier. They're friends with her boss."

"Yeah. Still. She seems far away from home."

It's clear that he doesn't just mean it in the geographical sense. I had that impression too, but now I almost feel like I should defend Kelli.

"She's careful. She's aware that it's a difficult subject for many here."

He doesn't answer but pours himself some coffee. We have always been close, comfortable in each other's company, but something is off tonight. I can't put my finger on it. Antsy. It must be the weather.

"You don't agree?"

He shrugs. "I don't know her. But the Gavin kid is bad news either way. The longer he stays missing, the more his parents will turn him into some sort of martyr. She better finds him soon."

Kelli said something similar earlier today.

"Yeah. I guess. You had a lot to do?"

"Just a few things to finish up for tomorrow," he answers vaguely.

It's not unusual that George goes back to his office after dinner. We both attended this school, and we are happy to work hard, give back to the community.

Erica's story was a shock for all of us. It has shaken our sense of safety. I'm afraid it did that for Fiona and her friends. I have no better explanation for them avoiding Erica for months. I can't believe they would abandon her over malicious rumors—or take part in them. I wish I could be of more help, to them, to Erica.

Maybe Kelli's presence will change something.

We can only hope.

Chapter Six

Kelli

I sleep badly, my mind crowded with conflicting theories and worries about where my inquiries might lead. Most of all I'm still baffled at the girls' reactions, and the way the adults around them seem to think it's no big deal. This town, so far, has been giving me nothing but a constant headache, though the dinner with Merin and her family was nice.

She's another enigma. A teacher, someone who seems to be concerned with the girls' safety, all of them, yet she buys into that idea that no one can stand up to the Gavins? Why?

I get a glimpse of the answer around six in the morning. I come out of the shower when my phone rings, and the next moment, my irate boss gives me a piece of his mind.

Do I even care anymore?

"Have you lost your mind?"

"I take it you talked to Mr. and Mrs. Gavin. Like everyone, they are telling me half-truths, and I'm no closer to figuring out where Lucas went. I'll check with the police station today."

I almost had him. I can sense some sort of surprised pause. Around here, everyone might be cowering to the Gavins, but I don't live here. Worst case scenario, I won't even go back to my job.

I can't be pressured.

"You accused their son of being a serial rapist, and them of covering up crimes."

That...is not entirely wrong.

"I didn't use those words," I try to defend myself anyway. "Given the context, it was important to know if Lucas had other run-ins with law enforcement. They have a lot of money and influence around here."

"And that's not for you to judge. I told you, all you are supposed to do is find Lucas, give them some peace."

"Like the peace Erica McQuade's family got?"

"The case has been tried," he says tersely.

"The more I learn, the more it seems like she was the one on trial. Not that it's such a surprise."

"Look, Jameson, there's a reason why I gave you this job. Do it. I don't want any more calls from the Gavins."

"Understood," I mumble, relieved when he hangs up. I dress and go down to the breakfast room, then change my mind and drive to the diner I saw the other day on main street. There's no particular timeline for when to meet with the sheriff. It might help me to pick up some small-town gossip.

I sit in a booth by the window and pick up the local newspaper from the table. Immediately, a waitress with an easy smile appears and fills a cup of coffee for me, informing me about the day's specials. I order a dish from the early bird menu that sounds decadent, a brioche toast with a fried egg, ham and cheese. There is something to be said about small town living, if it wasn't for all the bad stuff, like someone always being in your business. Gossip. I'm aware of the looks. People aren't that curious about one another in the city.

Lucas Gavin's disappearance is still a headline. I frown at the high school picture, showing him smiling, a "good boy." People go out of their way to make excuses for men like him, even and often those who should know better, because the alternative is too uncomfortable. The Ericas of this world pay the price. I toss the paper aside, not sure if I still have an appetite.

Taking a look around, I realize Merin Burke is here with an older woman, probably having breakfast before work. She doesn't notice me, so I study her, noticing her serious expression. Perhaps they are talking about the case too. The more you try to sweep something under the proverbial carpet, the more it keeps coming back to you.

I should know. I wouldn't be here if I had a choice, nothing to atone for.

Again, I notice the difference in the way she dresses for school, and at home. It's not just for being casual, it's almost like she's a different person at home. She's attractive either way.

I turn back to my coffee, suppressing a sigh. I don't need any more complications in my life, not that I'd ever consider messing with a married woman. In a town where everyone has guns.

I see a squad car drive by slowly, reminded that I still have a job to do, and the sooner it's finished the better.

Nothing's resolved yet. The bit of thunder and lightning we had yesterday did nothing to resolve the humid heat, and the newspaper's forecast warns of bigger things to come.

But I'll be back home by then.

❧

"Good morning," Merin greets me when she and her companion stop at my table on their way to the counter. "I see you found the place for the best breakfast in town."

"I thought it was the only place in town," I joke, realizing that the woman with Merin gives me a frown in return.

Merin is quick to change the subject.

"Louise, this is Kelli Jameson. Kelli, my colleague Louise."

"Nice to meet you."

I imagine that she might have heard a story or two about me, because the frown doesn't waver much. It makes me wonder what Merin's work environment is like, and if there's pressure on her to dress a decade off her age.

"Merin, could I talk to you for a second?"

"I'll go pay," Louise says with unveiled disapproval before she leaves us in relative privacy. I seize the moment.

"You already went out of your way having me for dinner yesterday, but...could I ask you another favor?"

"I'm afraid we're all out of pie already."

We both laugh.

"No, that's not it. Talking to you really helped me. I realize that people around here aren't too sure if they can trust me, for different reasons. I was hoping that you could talk to Fiona, see if she or her friends can remember anything that might help. The sooner I find Lucas, the sooner I can stop asking nosy questions, and go home."

She seems surprised at my request.

"I'm not sure if that will help you, but I can try. Fiona comes over at least once a week. Look, Kelli, I don't want you to get the wrong impression. They were all shaken over what happened to Erica."

"Why did they abandon her?"

"I don't know," she says, visibly troubled. "But if I learn anything, I'll let you know."

Under the stern looks of Louise, who has returned, she types her number into my phone.

"Thank you."

Merin hesitates before she asks, "You really think something happened to him?"

"He committed a crime. A lot of things could happen."

Neither of us is satisfied with the answer, but we both have to go back to our jobs.

~~~

The badge of the female officer at the front desk reads "Woodward." I remember I saw her at the bar the other night.

"Good morning, Officer," I greet her. "My name is Kelli Jameson. Could I speak to Sheriff Cross, please?"

"On what subject?"

"Lucas Gavin. Mr. and Mrs. Gavin hired me to investigate his disappearance. I understand they reported him missing to you first."

Her expression doesn't give anything away.

"I'll see if the sheriff is available."

"Thanks."

I'm not sure if they are going out of their way to be helpful, or if there's just so little to do in this town, but a few minutes later, I'm sitting in the sheriff's office. The smell of smoke is pervasive. This is probably not in compliance with regulations for government buildings, but who'd tell him?

"Thank you for meeting me," I say. "I won't take much of your time. I have talked to Lucas's parents, and they wish for me to investigate. Do you have any leads?"

"It's too bad that Mr. and Mrs. Gavin don't seem to trust us—"

"I don't think that's the case..."

He holds up a hand. "I know they're still mad we followed up on it when the McQuade girl filed charges. We had no choice."

"I understand. Regarding Lucas..."

"He dropped off the face of the earth," he says. "His phone is turned off. Last sign of life, as you certainly know, was the call to his friend. Lucas was staying with his parents. He had breakfast with them, five days ago, and no one has seen him since."

"No one."

"That's what I said."

"Isn't that strange? You'd think after such a high-profile case, people would still pay attention?"

"He's a local boy. People mind their own business." Was he actually bristling?

"But no one has seen him in five days? You think he left town?"

"Could be? We contacted his friends right away, but they hadn't heard from him, except for Kyle."

"You talked to Pete Bradley?" He still hasn't called me back.

"He was out of town for his cousin's wedding."

"Okay. Sheriff, I know that if there are any other records, they would likely be sealed because of his age at the time, but is it possible that Lucas got into trouble before? That someone felt they needed to hold him accountable this time?"

"If that's the case, I don't know anything about it."

"Was Lucas seeing anyone?"

"I'm not aware either. Is this all, Ms. Jameson?"

"At this moment, yes. Thank you for your time."

Chapter Seven

Time. The timeline is all messed up. It would have made more sense for Lucas to disappear right after he was accused of rape. The trial is over, he got off, and obviously a lot of people sided with him. Why would he run? Is there something bigger to come? Did Kyle Vance lie to my face?

Did the girls?

And what if they told the truth? I don't want to go back to the possibility that Erica's father might have to do something with Lucas' disappearance.

After my meeting with the sheriff, I get in the car and drive around. The Gavins' next-door neighbors barely deserve that term as their houses are far apart. The Gavins' is by far the most luxurious. I imagine Lucas talking to Kyle on the phone, no doubt vilifying Erica, or the next girl, then—what? Did he decide to go out? Meet someone—whom? Did somebody lure him into a trap?

This little town in the middle of nowhere has a lot of wide-open spaces. It's hard to imagine that no one saw him. Between the parents' property and the next houses to the west, there's a stretch of forest. The police and volunteers have been searching, I know.

Nothing.

I drive past the school again, then find myself close to the Collins' house, and by proxy, Merin's. I make a U-turn, as I have no good reason to see her again. I'm not even sure she has any intention of keeping her promise and talking to Erica's friends.

Yes, she's been nice to me and all, and the situation is puzzling, but perhaps I should leave it at that: Mean girls. Teenagers who look out for themselves.

Except...if the Gavins' influence reaches even further than the obvious. Did they pressure those girls, or anyone, for that matter, not to support Erica?

Back in town, I stop at the diner once more for a coffee—because there isn't any other place on main street—and I write down, *check parents' jobs*. I can't believe I didn't think of this earlier. The Gavins run a big business, farm machinery and supplies. Jobs aren't plentiful in this town.

I check my watch. Merin is probably still in class, but I could call her later. Or I drop by the girls' houses again.

Lexi Adams lives closest. Lucky for me, she's home already, if not much cooperative.

"I told you already, we don't know what happened to Lucas. Why can't you leave us alone?"

Her parents aren't home. She's watching her younger sister who's playing with blocks on the floor.

"I'm still trying to figure it out," I say. "You went to school with Erica, you saw her every day. You really think she lied?"

"What difference does it make? The judge didn't really care about what we thought. Besides, we weren't there."

"You've known Erica for years. You must have an opinion."

"See, this is exactly why we decided to keep our distance. The police, reporters, everyone kept asking questions we couldn't answer."

"Couldn't...or someone told you not to say anything?"

She stares back at me morosely.

"What the hell does that mean?"

"You tell me, Lexi. The Gavins are one of the biggest employers around here. Your parents both work for them?"

"That doesn't change anything. I can't tell you what I don't know."

"So, no one approached you and told you to withdraw support for Erica?"

"No. Is that all? I have homework to do."

"That's all, thank you."

I go back to my car and wait.

Minutes later, Lexi leaves the house with her little sister in tow. She straps her into the car seat and then takes the road to the city.

I follow her at a distance.

She meets Amanda at the diner. I wish I knew what they were talking about.

<hr />

The sun is setting, but there's no sign of cooling down yet. Resigning to the fact that I'm not going to learn much more tonight, I finally drive out to the bar sporting the rainbow flag. There's a motel not far where I book a room—not because I want to hook up with anyone, but because I want to have a drink or two, and I don't want to drive home afterwards.

This motel is the first on the way out of town. Following a hunch, I show a picture of Lucas to the teen behind the counter. He shakes his head.

Whatever.

I make the short walk to the bar, and, after stepping over its threshold, take a deep breath. It's still fairly early, most of the chairs unoccupied. It's dark, but clean, and the air conditioning is on full blast. I intend to spend some time here.

I haven't gone into much detail with the people in town, but given how the trial ended, I can imagine what many of them think of this place, or the people who frequent it. I don't envy anyone living in this town who has to keep secrets to keep their job or not be shunned by their neighbors. I couldn't imagine a life like that. Even staying for a week, I feel like the walls are closing in.

In here, it's a welcome time-out.

The blue-haired bartender sets a beer in front of me, and I almost sigh in relief.

"New in town?" she asks, sounding sympathetic.

"Just passing through," I say. "I don't intend to stay."

"That's too bad for us." She smiles, and I smile back at her, though this is where it ends. Much too young. I turn around to the room, realizing that it's starting to fill up.

"You've been working here a long time?"

Her eyes narrow. "Are you a cop?"

"PI, but I'm not working now. I needed a break from...the sun."

She gives a knowing smile. "Don't we all? Have a good time."

It's most inappropriate, but I think of Merin. Why do I always make my life so much more complicated than it needs to be?

⁂

At the bar, I'm among strangers, just as I am in town, but the feeling is completely different. For me anyway, because it's a reminder that I can go whenever I please. I overhear bits and pieces of conversations that tell me it's not like that for everyone. A cute blonde comes on to me, and for a split-second I wonder...

No, I'm here to do a job. All I wanted was a moment to breathe, to go to a place where I don't have to explain or justify.

I'll figure something out. Go home.

Forget about the married woman who makes a damn good strawberry pie.

I am about to leave my motel room in the morning when I see the man in the parking lot getting into this car.

I recognize him: Kyle Vance. There's another man with him. I don't get a clear look, but what are the odds that this could be Pete Bradley? What are they up to? I don't like the idea of two entitled men who have already covered up a crime, this close to a gay bar.

I mull this over on my drive back, mostly because it helps me chase thoughts of Merin out of my head.

I have considered that Lucas's disappearance might be a result of vigilante justice. If Erica's dad wasn't involved, another victim's friend or family member might be. But what if someone close to him wished him harm? What if Lucas told the truth, and he was a witness, not the perpetrator?

No. I have to backtrack a bit. At that party, Erica went into the room with Lucas, according to everyone involved. This is where the stories start to differ. I still believe her, but what if Kyle and Pete had a reason for wanting Lucas to disappear? He might have wanted to go to the police, change his statement, implicate them? Too many theories, with not much to support any of them.

Merin didn't call me back either.

Perhaps I should have given that cute blonde a chance.

Chapter Eight

I t's hot. As I drive back to my hotel, I wonder if I should have brought more clothes. I hadn't planned on doing laundry here, but I might not be able to avoid it.

Back in town, I spend much of the rest of the day in my hotel room, using the spotty Wi-Fi to comb through social media profiles, for any hint of where Lucas might have gone. Like the last time I checked, the Internet is full of outlandish conspiracy theories. Blaming Erica and her family. One poster points out that everyone had an alibi for pretty much the entire day.

No, this would be too easy. I like the idea of the "good boy" club turning on one another, better. The problem is, I don't have any more proof for it than the conspiracy theorists have for theirs.

For dinner, I choose the bar on main street once more. The female cop, Woodward, dressed in civilian clothes, is sitting at a table with a man I assume to be her boyfriend or husband.

Merin and George are sitting at another.

He waves when he recognizes me, and with some reluctance, I walk over to them. He probably doesn't know that I involved his wife in some of my inquiries.

He sure as hell doesn't know about other thoughts I've been having about his wife, not that it matters. It's not like she's interested.

Even if she was, there's no way, is there?

"Hey," I say. "Teachers out on a school night, what's the world coming to?"

"Just having dinner," he returns with a good-natured smile. "How's your investigation coming along?"

"It's coming along," I say vaguely.

"Would you like to sit with us?"

What is that supposed to mean?

"I don't want to disturb you on your night out."

"Oh no, you're not," he says. "Right, Merin?

"No, you're not disturbing us." Her smile is polite, but I detect a hint of unease in her tone.

"All right, then. Thank you. Perhaps you could recommend something from the menu."

I'm not sure I understand the dynamics here, but I sit. So far, I haven't been able to get much traction. The two of them have lived here for years. I might be learning something by listening carefully to what they say...

"That, and so far, you've only learned the worst of our home-town," George says. "We hope to show you that we're not de-fined by one, albeit horrible, crime."

"Much is defined by the Gavins' wealth though, isn't it? I hear they employ a good portion of the town."

He shrugs. "That doesn't mean they own anyone, or that there aren't good people here."

"Running away isn't always the best option," Merin ads.

She can't know, but I feel judged. After all, I couldn't wait to get out of the town I was born in—not quite as depressing as this one, but too small all the same.

"As long as people can make that choice. You have a lovely home, with a breathtaking view, and your jobs are here."

"I can't imagine living anywhere else," Merin says. "George is right, what happened doesn't define us. There's so much more to this community."

Strawberry pie. Endless farmland. Still not enough in my opinion, but I imagine they care about the kids they teach.

"You have family here, besides your sister?"

"Both our parents still live here," she says. "Born and raised." She laughs a little. "They'd be horrified if I hadn't come back to teach here after college."

"Horrified is a big word," George's tone is mildly scolding, and she looks at her hands. "We both wanted to give back."

"So, you've known each other for a long time."

"Oh yes. High school sweethearts," he confirms. "We went to different colleges, but not far away. We always came back for the holidays, and we were lucky that when we graduated, we both had job offers on the table."

This is bizarre, me, at the table with them, talking about these rather private issues. I can't stay away.

"What about you?" he asks.

"Me? I guess you could say single and looking. Just like with Lucas, I haven't had much luck lately."

I'm not sure if that's a good joke, or any joke at all, but they smile politely. I catch Merin's gaze on me. I wish I knew what she was thinking.

"I haven't given up hope yet, that the right woman is out there," I say, gauging their reactions. Only a split-second of hesitation.

"I'm sure she is," George agrees.

Merin's smile is a bit forced, or perhaps that's my imagination.

Mixing alcohol and emotions with business is not a good idea, but at least I remember to ask them about Kyle and Pete.

"You must be mistaken," Merin says. "Pete Bradley hasn't been in town since the trial."

"He has a reason to hide?"

"Well, like Kyle, he's associated with Lucas, and the accusations. Hiding, I don't know."

"When people realize they can get away with criminal behavior, when there's always someone to bail them out, they don't stop," I argue. "They don't try it just once."

I can tell they're uncomfortable.

"The town wasn't on trial, Lucas was." Merin speaks with surprising heat. "Why do I have the feeling you think we're all the same, that we could just be silent and cover up something this horrible? It seems like you're blaming my niece and her friends more than the guy who did it."

"Merin." George sounds self-conscious. "Let's not rehash this now."

"I'm not blaming you, or anyone but Lucas. But he's gone, and he must have had some help—if he left town freely."

"Fiona has nothing to do with any of it. This has been hard on them. Can't you understand that? No one wants to think that this could happen—" She stops, shaking her head. "To someone they care about."

"But it did, and ignoring it only makes it worse. I'm sorry, to the both of you. I didn't mean to ruin your evening."

"No, that's fine. We're just talking, right? Truth be told, we've been wondering what happened, not just with Lucas," George admits. "Fiona, Amanda, and Lexi, they used to be tight with Erica. Only goes to show what kind of impact a crime like this has."

Merin has gone silent. All of a sudden, it makes sense to me. I don't know if George is aware, at this moment or in general.

I wish he wasn't here. I wish I didn't have to push good people when I honestly don't care what happened to Lucas. He's the bad guy here.

I am certain that Erica wasn't the only victim, but maybe Lucas isn't the only perpetrator.

What a messed-up place. However, I'm not oblivious to the fact that it's an attitude you can find anywhere. The question is how much space and importance it is given. It all depends on how much people are willing to indulge and coddle. *Boys will be boys.* Rich boys, society is willing to look the other way.

I am in luck: George gets to his feet. "I'll be right back," he says and heads for the restroom.

Merin regards me with a resigned expression.

"You're getting the wrong idea," she says. "About everything."

"Am I? You're right, no one wants to think that it could happen to someone we love—or ourselves. But it does, right? And rich parents and expensive lawyers make it go away, until the next time."

"No, it wasn't like that," she says, exasperated.

"You don't have to tell me. You're right, it has nothing to do with Lucas."

"Everyone who has worked for the Gavins has a story of unwelcome jokes, and inappropriate comments. We always brushed it off."

"Your sister?"

Merin nods. "My sister, her friends. Lately, we've been wondering, if we had done anything differently, if we said something...Perhaps all of this could have been avoided."

"No. None of it is your fault, or your sister's, or Erica's. I thought that the parents might have covered up more of Lucas's crimes before, but it's more like father like son, right? Are you sure it stopped at inappropriate comments? Did anybody ever involve the police?"

This is a different dimension. It's even worse than I thought. I can't help wondering if Merin has a story, and I'm already invested in the outcome.

"Not for this. With the kind of accusations Erica made, they had no choice. I shouldn't be telling you any of this."

"You can talk to me." I reach out to touch her hand but abort the impulse before making contact. "I'm so sorry, Merin, for all of this. My hope is that if I can find Lucas, there's still a way to hold him accountable. And maybe his family."

"You don't know what you're up against. Didn't you say that your boss is a friend of Mr. Gavin's?"

"I'm not married to that job," I say, noticing her flinch. "All I want is to find the truth." When she doesn't answer, I say, "You could always leave here."

She shakes her head. "You don't get it. I can't."

George returns at this moment. I reach for my glass and take a hasty sip. I almost made a huge mistake, came this close to behaving inappropriately myself. Wanting the touch to mean more than it did. Telling her what to do.

I need to get out of here, and not just this restaurant.

⁂

So being an asshole runs in the Gavin family, not that it's a big surprise. I'm still pondering these revelations, and the reasons why Pete Bradley came to town.

Are he and Kyle plotting something?

I have been back in my hotel room for an hour or so when a sharp knock on the door jolts me out of my thoughts.

I open the door to Merin who walks inside and starts pacing without so much as a greeting. I know we left some unfinished business, but I didn't realize how important it was for her to set the record straight.

"I need you to stay away from my family," she says. "You are making everything worse."

"That's a pretty broad statement. You want to elaborate on that?"

Merin halts, as if gathering her thoughts. "You said it yourself, it's not our fault. Ellen needs that job. And I...my family is here. All my life is here. And I hate the Gavins and their spawn for hurting all of us. Are you happy now?"

"I didn't mean to hurt you," I say softly. "I want to help."

"You're not helping."

I'm aware I'm walking a fine line, and I have no excuse. If the high school sweethearts living in the beautiful home, with no kids, have no chemistry, it's none of my business. It doesn't mean anything. It doesn't have to.

"Then tell me how I can do better."

She'll be innocent in this. All the blame will be on me. I reach out and brush my fingertips over her cheek. Merin is still under my touch, her eyes wide. She doesn't step away or slap me, and I lean in.

She all but jumps back before my lips touch hers, and laughs. "This is how you're helping? That's funny."

"I'm sorry."

"Are you?" she challenges.

"Yes. I swear. You don't need any of this."

"You're right I don't. And I'll give you some advice. Here is not a good place to look for love. People are old-fashioned. I'm not saying it's right, but..." She looks to her feet. "I don't want you to get hurt either. I wish I could help you. I wish I could make things better for Erica, or the other girls. We're all feeling tired and helpless."

"One family shouldn't have this much power."

"I agree. But what can we do?"

At least, she's looking at me again, and she doesn't seem to be mad at me. I'm not sure if that's better or worse.

"Do you think the police properly investigated the rape?"

"I can't say otherwise. They brought in an investigator from the county. The case went to trial after all."

"It's a small town. Do you know if any of the sheriff's relatives work for Gavin?" At this point, I wouldn't put anything past them. "See, if the trial was a sham, Lucas's disappearance is probably related."

"Then you have to ask the Gavins about it."

"I know. But they're stonewalling like everyone else."

"I'm so tired. Everyone is." I'm startled to see tears in her eyes. This time, I don't hesitate, and pull her close to me. Doubts be damned, this feels right. We both need someone we can trust.

"We can help each other figure this out," I say, sounding more confident than I feel. "No one should be living like this. Someone has to stop them, hold them accountable. For the next girl, at the next party."

Merin leans into me for a long moment before she steps back.

"Lucas always had a mean streak. I hope he doesn't come back."

In that case, I'll have to leave soon, and I'm shocked to realize I'm not sure if I want to.

I have one last lead to follow: Pete Bradley.

"I need to go," Merin says. "I'm sure George wonders where I am."

"Do you love him?"

We both know she doesn't owe me an answer. Merin turns to leave.

Chapter Nine

I ask around, but no one has seen Pete in town. That seems to be the standard answer for everything, no one sees or knows anything. *Sorry, I can't help you.* Another sweltering afternoon.

I step into a small supermarket to get some more water when I become aware of the whispers. It takes me a moment to realize that the two women, one of them Louise the geography teacher, aren't talking about me. At the other end of the isle, Erica McQuade is pushing a cart, her shoulders hunched.

"Hi, Erica."

Out of the corner of my eye, I see Louise and her friend turn away slightly, as if they didn't want me to catch them staring. Does anyone here really care?

Erica barely looks at me.

"You're still here."

"Yes, I am. This must get old pretty fast," I say, referring to the gossiping women.

"After some time, you don't hear it anymore."

I can't argue with that. But I need to make some headway, push the issue so the day when I can leave town is coming sooner than later.

What the hell was I thinking?

"You heard that Pete is in town?"

She halts abruptly, turns to me. The color has drained from her face.

"What does that mean?"

"I wish I knew, but no one's telling me the whole story. I saw him with Kyle. That must have something to do with Lucas's disappearance, don't you think?"

Erica shakes her head. "Why do you care what I think? No one else does."

I catch a glance at her empty cart.

"I do. I promise. Can I buy you an ice cream?"

"Why would you want to do that? I answered your questions."

"I know. I just think you might be able to help me. I swear I won't ask you about the party."

"Because you're uncomfortable with the subject?"

She's not wrong.

"Because there's no need. Please? I could use one myself."

Erica finally agrees. It comes as no surprise that people stare at us, on the street, at the ice cream parlor. I wonder if I'm going to get another angry call from my boss, but I don't care.

"I'm sure they know where Lucas is," Erica says when we sit in a corner booth, finally shielded from curious gazes and whispers. "I don't know names, but there were other girls at the school...They always lied for him."

I think of what Merin told me. Maybe the world has gone insane, or maybe it's always been that way, and we were just too naïve to see it, or too scared to admit it.

"Lucas seems to have a bunch of people cleaning up his messes. His friends, his parents...I heard that Lexi's parents work for the Gavins."

"A lot of people do," she says with a shrug.

"Did anybody pressure them to keep their distance?"

"It's possible. It doesn't really make much of a difference for me. People will always look at me and think..." She doesn't finish the sentence. She doesn't have to.

"No one can force you to spend the rest of your life here if you don't want to."

What the hell is it with people and this town?

"Maybe. I'm not sure where I'd go."

Anywhere but here would be an instant improvement, but I don't say that out loud. It wouldn't be news to Erica, and she has enough on her plate as it is. I wish there was a way I could take her somewhere no one would harass her while she's buying groceries. Well. You could argue that's exactly what I did.

"I know that Kyle lives in an apartment his parents probably paid for. They spent the night in a motel. Around here, where would Pete go? Do you know if his parents live in town?"

"The biggest house aside from the Gavins'? They invested in oil or something. It's close to the exit."

"Thank you, Erica. It's important that I talk to him too. Perhaps his parents can tell me where I find him."

"Be careful," she says, all of a sudden apprehensive.

"Because of his parents?"

"No, they're just clueless. Pete...He carries a knife."

Her words open up a world of possibilities even more horrible than what we already know.

"That's all right. I have a gun," I say grimly. We sit in silence for a few seconds before I break my earlier promise. "Is there anything you didn't tell the police?"

"No. I told them everything I knew then, and again, when Lucas went missing, and they came to my house. That's all I can tell you, and I still have to do the freaking groceries. Can I?"

"Yes. Of course."

We leave together, and I get in my car to pay the Bradleys a visit.

It makes me uneasy to think of why Erica felt like she needed to mention the knife.

I've had enough of the stonewalling and lies, and so I find myself parked behind the wall on a lot close to the driveway leading up to the Bradleys' estate. Damn the wide-open spaces—there isn't much space to hide, but I can't let him get away this time.

Rich kids, expensive lawyers, there's a pattern. If he's in town, he will show up here at some point.

And I need to do something other than obsess over the fact that I owe Merin an apology. Just because I find her attractive, because I don't want her to be tied down by the ridiculous conventions of this town, it's not my place to tell her what to do.

She chose this life, here, with a man who seems more like a good friend than a lover. Just because I want her, it doesn't mean that this doesn't work for her. Some couples are like that. End of story.

If only it rained more than a few drops at night. I hate feeling sticky and dusty the moment I get out of a shower.

Perhaps I need to call my boss and tell him it's over, I failed. What was supposed to be a quick, easy gathering of information, has turned into a painful tug of war.

It takes me a few hours of feeling sorry for myself before Pete shows up. He arrives alone, and judging from the time he spends inside, he's having dinner with his parents. It's getting dark—better for me.

He comes back out around nine, gets in his car and drives away. I follow at a distance. He has talked to Kyle after I visited the latter, but never called me back. There's a reason for that. I'm going to ask him those questions.

The drive is about twenty-five minutes and leads to a more forested area. There are no houses here. Is he meeting someone?

Lucas?

All of a sudden, the thought of the gun in the glove compartment is very comforting.

He parks close to a clearing, and I slowly drive by, find a spot not too exposed and then hurry back.

Pete Bradley walks with brisk steps. He halts when I step on a small branch.

"Who's there?" he asks, more irritated than worried. I hold my breath, and he walks on.

After another few minutes, Pete stops and checks his watch. He turns his attention towards a sound, this time not from me. I turn around as well, expecting Kyle Vance to show up...

It's not Kyle walking out of the shadows, but Fiona Collins.

I shouldn't be surprised. I inch a bit closer to them to make out their words. She has her arms wrapped around herself even though it's not cold. At a closer look, I can tell he's angry.

"She's asking everyone, okay?" Fiona says, obviously referring to me. "I don't know where Lucas is. I thought you did."

"He's my friend. If you did something—"

"What the hell are you talking about? What would I do?"

"Hell if I know." He steps closer to her, and she stares back at him defiantly. "I thought I could trust you," he adds. That is interesting. "But if you turn on me, remember what happened to Erica."

"I don't need to turn on anyone. Lucas is a liar, and you know it. He's even playing you. Pathetic."

"I'm going to show you who's pathetic!" He pushes her up against a tree, his hand around her neck.

I've seen enough. The next moments are all about instinct, and he's face down on the ground, my gun pointed at him. Fiona stares at the scene in shock.

"Mr. Bradley," I say. "We finally meet. I guess the police will want to ask you some questions first."

After I call the station, two male officers pick him up. Sheriff Cross arrives with them, surveying the scene with something akin to apprehension.

"Let's go to the station, and you can call your parents from there," he tells Fiona who's been eerily quiet. "Ms. Jameson, would you please come with us? I need to ask you a few questions as well."

"Sure. I have a license."

"I assumed you would. Let's go."

In the back of the car, Fiona doesn't talk to me. She stares out the window, avoiding any communication. As bad as this is, I feel somewhat relieved—this situation could have turned out much worse. Now, I might have given the police, and myself, a lead regarding Lucas.

Pete Bradley's threats were basically an admission to what we all know, that Lucas lied about Erica. But for anyone to hold him accountable this time, we must find him first. Why would Pete think that Fiona did anything?

I think back to what Merin told me about her sister. She, too, might have been harassed by Gavin senior. I'll have to tread carefully.

Chapter Ten

A t the station, Cross takes Fiona to an office to call her parents, and Bradley to another one. I end up in an interrogation room with a male officer called LeBlanc. I've seen him with Woodward before.

"You don't have a lot of space here, do you?" If that's a joke, it falls flat. "Really, an interrogation room?"

"Sheriff Cross tells me you have a license for that gun?"

"Yes, of course." I hand him the paperwork.

"Why were you there in the first place?"

How long of a story does he want?

"Mr. Bradley threatened Ms. Collins. He referred to Erica McQuade, saying that the same might happen to her."

"From the beginning, please."

I suppress a sigh and start over as ordered. "You might have heard that Mr. and Mrs. Gavin hired me to find Lucas. I talked to his friend Kyle Vance, left a message for Mr. Bradley, but he didn't call me back. Then—"

I remember only now that the reason I saw Kyle and Pete together was that I spent the night in a motel close to a gay bar. I don't want the officer to know in case he thinks that takes away any weight from my words.

"Then what?"

"I heard that Bradley was in town, so I went to see his parents. They weren't forthcoming, so I decided to stake out the route to their estate. Pete arrived, stayed with them for a while, and then he drove to the woods. The rest, you need to ask Fiona Collins."

"Oh, I think that's where it gets most interesting." Neither of us noticed Sheriff Cross coming inside. "I can take over for a second," he says.

With a shrug, Officer LeBlanc gets up and leaves the room.

"Have Fiona's parents arrived?" I ask. "She should see a doctor. She was in shock."

"We'll see to it that all is taken care of. Right now, I'm having a hard time convincing Pete not to file charges against you, Ms. Jameson."

"What?"

"I was hoping you could help me with that."

"What else do you need? He attacked the girl, choked her, and threatened her with rape. I intervened."

"Lucky for her," he acknowledges. "Look, those boys have caused enough trouble for this town. I don't want any more of that."

"Good. Then we're on the same page. I assume you're going to charge him."

"We're still figuring that out."

"You need my statement, let me know."

"Sure. Thank you, Ms. Jameson. You can go now."

I hesitate. I'm not sure if I can trust him, and I'm definitely not here to make his life easier, but they might have resources that I don't.

"He knows something, if not about Lucas's whereabouts, then about the fact that Lucas lied. There's something to learn from him."

"Thanks for the advice." He gets up and motions for me to do the same.

"You're not going to let him go, right?"

"We'll do what we can," Sheriff Cross says, sounding much too cryptic for my comfort. "Go home now, lay low. This is how you can help the most."

I would have been okay with a simple *thank you*.

⁂

When I go to my car, I see Fiona leaving with her parents. There's another vehicle, and I don't recognize it right away.

"Kelli!" Merin calls.

I halt, unsure what I can or should say to her. She gets out of the car, and for a few seconds, we stand in front of each other in silence.

"I'm so sorry," I finally say. "I hope Fiona will be okay." When she doesn't answer, I continue, "and I owe you an apology. Where you live, with whom, it's none of my business. I just wish these damn people didn't have so much power."

I'm not even sure who I'm talking about any longer. The Gavins, the Bradleys, and their offspring? People openly gossiping about others?

"Yeah. We all wish that. At least the police are looking into this now. And you don't owe me an apology. You misunderstood, that's all."

Misunderstood what? My own feelings? Or something we both can't admit? Nothing has changed as to her marital status though, and I have to respect that.

"I guess that sums it up. Drive safely," I say, for the lack of something better.

"You too."

I get in my car and drive straight to the bar, almost hoping that the cute blonde is there again.

She's not, but that's okay. I'm here for a different kind of denial.

···

It's late. I should go back to the motel—it's that or sleep in my car. I just want to forget about everything I've been dealing with for a few more hours. The fact that Bradley will be out soon. Merin's polite but undeniable rebuke. My repeated failure.

All I've done so far is stir up painful truths for the women in town, without doing anything to help them, or move the case forward. Maybe I was too hard on the girls, on everyone.

But people like the Gavins can't pull strings forever, especially if they are involved in something criminal. It needs to stop somewhere.

On my third or fourth beer, I turn around, and my jaw drops. I quickly make myself as small as possible. The two men kissing passionately at the far end of the room haven't noticed me—and I want to keep it that way. One, I don't recognize.

The other one is George Burke, Merin's husband. Making out with another man in a gay bar.

I toss a few bills on the counter, cast one more look at the couple, and leave, my emotions all over the place. Okay, so I had too much to drink, but there's so much more to it. *I* misunderstood? There I had a guilty conscience for thinking about Merin, for wondering what if, while George is cheating on her.

This freaking town is built on lies and hypocrisy.

···

The same teen as before, looking like he was pitying me, hands me the key to a room.

The next morning, the ringing of my cell phone wakes me. My hang-over pity party induced headache has my brain in a vice. I fumble for the phone on the nightstand, but don't make it in time.

There's a voicemail from Sheriff Cross, to come by the station as soon as possible.

A text message from Merin. *Can we talk?*

I wonder if all of this has to do with Bradley's arrest and anything he revealed afterwards.

After a quick shower, I dress. I intend to go back to town immediately, but I need a strong coffee first. A bucket thereof, maybe.

I stop at the first restaurant I see. To my relief, the smell of food is not making me sick, on the contrary. Changing plans, I sit at one of the tables and order breakfast. I think Sheriff Cross can wait a few minutes.

Merin...I need to think carefully about how this conversation is going to go. I have no illusions about what's going on here. It would be hard for George in this town to be openly gay, or bi, for that matter, and keep his job as football coach.

People talk, people are cruel when it comes to prejudice. That much I understand. But Merin, she doesn't deserve this. She has to know, even if she's going to hate the messenger. This is not about me, but him potentially putting her at risk. The longer I think about this, the angrier I am, at him, at this horrible place where people have been conditioned to ignore the truth, no matter who gets hurt.

Part of it might be hunger, I realize when the waitress sets my plate in front of me, eggs, potatoes, toast, and a side of pancakes, I could kiss her in gratitude. As I dig in, my gaze falls onto the TV on the wall. At the same moment, I realize that most patrons' attention has gone to the coverage of a local TV station.

It shows a lake close to where Bradley assaulted Fiona last night.

A couple of teens who went out on a boat made a grisly discovery: A dead body.

I know before anyone says it out loud: The dead man is Lucas Gavin.

All of a sudden, I no longer have an appetite, and I'm not sure I want to know why Sheriff Cross wants to see me.

Chapter Eleven

T he town is unusually busy. There's a TV crew, squad cars circling, and your usual onlookers. I assume they'll bring Lucas's body to the county morgue.

I have many mixed emotions about this development. How did Lucas die? Did he go out on the lake, get drunk or high, and fall in? Did someone push him? There's another explanation, that he was killed somewhere else, and someone dumped him in the water. Someone strong enough to move a body. Someone angry enough to want to kill.

I hope Mr. McQuade's alibi holds. Everything else would be an even bigger catastrophe. I want to talk to Merin even more, but the sheriff is expecting me for a reason.

He's standing at the front desk with Woodward when I arrive.

"Ms. Jameson. Please come with me."

Back to the interrogation room. It's starting to become unpleasant.

"I heard about Lucas. I guess you notified the parents?"

"I have," he confirms.

At least they didn't learn about it from the news.

"I'm meeting them again this afternoon," Sheriff Cross adds.

"Could I come with you? I assume they will want to talk to me." I can't help but wince, thinking of the last conversation we've had. Damn. Even though my theories have gone in all kinds of directions, I'm still alarmed by the latest development.

Well, boss, I found him. Can I go home?

"It would be better if you stayed away from them for the moment. They are grieving, and I guess they'll no longer need your services. We'll work with the county's Homicide unit."

"Homicide?" I sit up straighter. "That's for certain already?"

"I guess it's unlikely he went out on the lake and shot himself," Sheriff Cross says dryly. "Ms. Jameson, I'm sure you understand that after what happened yesterday, we need to rule out your gun as the murder weapon."

"Murder weapon?" My voice rises a few notches. "What are you talking about? Lucas Gavin was already missing when I came to town. His parents hired me."

"Yes, and it seems you were socializing with Erica McQuade's family and the Burkes instead of doing what you were hired to do. People saw you in town with Erica."

"I bought her an ice cream. You can't seriously think I had something to do with this?"

"It doesn't matter what I think. I'd like to rule you out as a suspect, and I believe that would be in both our interests."

"I have nothing to hide."

"Good. I'm glad we have an understanding."

When I can finally leave, my first call is to the person responsible for my presence here. He agrees that it will be for the better if I don't contact the Gavins.

"So, this is it?"

"Keep your eyes and ears open, see if you can find anything."

"He's dead. Whoever did it, not my problem."

"I'll pretend I didn't hear that. Remember what we agreed to? You do your job. Then you come home."

"Yes sir." I suppress a sigh. In a way, my life isn't so different from Merin's, or any of the women in town. I'm trapped here just the same.

"You know that they call this place tornado alley. I was hoping I could avoid seeing one."

"Stay away from the windows," he instructs, and hell if there isn't a double meaning to that.

Next, I call Merin. She doesn't pick up. I leave her a message to tell her I'm on my way. Twenty minutes later, I knock on her front door, and she opens it, looking worried.

"Are you alone?"

"Yes. I guess you heard...about Lucas?"

"Yes, I spoke to the sheriff earlier." I don't tell her about all the implications. Should I? Isn't there anything else I need to tell her?

"Come on in. Would you like a glass of iced tea?"

There's a lot more I would like. "Sure, that sounds great."

She serves it in tall glasses, and we sit in the living room under the soft whirr of the ceiling fan.

"I don't know how to feel," she confesses. "I know he did something horrible, but this is still..."

"Bad. It's bad either way," I finish for her. "The police might want to look at Erica's father again." Or, for some inexplicable reason, me.

"It's already a strange day," she says, holding my gaze.

I can't lie to her.

"There's something I need to tell you."

I won't be part of the investigation. That means no matter what anyone says, my days as a visitor are counted. And once I leave, I might never see her again. "Please, hear me out. I...I might have given you mixed signals, and I'm sorry."

I sit on the couch with her, aware of her deer-in-the-head-lights expression.

"I understand you don't see a way out right now, but it doesn't have the be like that."

"My family is here. My whole life." I notice she doesn't mention George first, and that's for a reason too.

I reach out to touch her hand, exhilarated when she doesn't pull back. If last night and today has taught me anything, it's that life is short and can change in a heartbeat.

"Maybe there could be a life elsewhere," I say, and lean in. Even now, she doesn't move, and I kiss her softly. I can't remember the last time such a chaste kiss had me this excited. To hell with all those powerful families who think they can dictate other people's lives. Here, maybe. Not where I'm from.

Merin sits still, her expression serene. Beautiful. She's not mad at me, and that has to count for something...but she didn't kiss me back either.

"It's an illusion," she says. "Everything about you is so tempting, but I can't do this."

"Why not?"

"Because I am married!"

Maybe that's a good enough reason even if I didn't know what I know. There's no way to avoid uncomfortable conversations and cutting ties.

"I get that..."

"Do you?"

"Merin, I went to a gay bar the other night."

"Let's not do this."

"Maybe you know the one, just out of town, off the road..."

"Stop."

"I'm so sorry. I saw George there, with another man. I understand that you don't want to be cheating, but he already is. You don't owe him anything."

Perhaps it was a tad too self-righteous of me to think I had figured it all out. I seem to be doing a lousy job at reading people lately. Maybe I deserve it all, this town, the case, rejection.

But I think she deserves to know.

"George isn't cheating on me," Merin says calmly. "I know he's seeing someone."

My jaw drops a bit. And I still don't get it.

"But how...?" None of my business. "Forget about it. You don't owe me any answers. I just want you to be safe."

"Why is that?" she asks, sounding genuinely interested.

"Because I care about you."

Merin doesn't dispute the truth of my statement.

"I understand where you're coming from, but I can assure you, you don't have to worry about me. You're right, I don't owe you answers. I want to try anyway—George and I had sex once, shortly after we got married. We were drunk. It was awkward. As you can see, I'm perfectly safe, and he's not irresponsible."

I take a sip of iced tea. I don't know what to say. In fact, I could think of a lot of things to say, but I'm sure she doesn't want to hear any of them.

"It's not just about his actions. Prejudiced people can be dangerous. If the school found out, they would likely find a way to fire him," I conclude. "They could come after you too. It's a big sacrifice for a job."

"For someone's livelihood? It's not as bad as you might think. We grew up here. This community means a lot to us, and we're friends. I don't think of it as a sacrifice."

Perhaps I need to accept that she'll never see it my way and move on. I can't stop myself.

"What if *you* meet someone?"

"You mean you? You come here for a week or two, stir things up and leave?" There's a world of emotions behind the sarcasm.

"What if it was more than that?"

"I can't leave, you won't stay. That answers the question, doesn't it?"

"So, you'll just carry on? He'll keep seeing men, you'll meet women in a discreet setting?"

I'm rude and provocative, on purpose. It's infuriating to see people who are trapped, and still make excuses for those who hold them hostage. It's not Merin I'm mad at, or even George. I wish they could see that they owe nothing to their toxic neighbors. Community my ass. I want to swear in a way that would make the whispering ladies in the supermarket blush with indignation.

I want to hit something.

"I haven't," Merin says, and all of a sudden, my anger seems meaningless. "I don't know what you're thinking, but I have my job, my friends, the house...Where would I even go?" She shakes her head with a sigh. "This is going nowhere, isn't it? You don't need to feel sorry for me. Let me ask you something, Kelli—if you have all the options where you live, if that's such a better place, why are you so unhappy?"

To my alarm, her words hit home. "That has nothing to do with me being a lesbian," I feel the need to clarify. "I've had some problems on the job. That's why they sent me here, to find Lucas, as a favor to the Gavins. Like you said, all I did was stir things up, and I hate it. I still believe Erica, and if her father shot Lucas, I wouldn't want him to go to prison for it. You're right, Merin. I could never live in this place."

As she mulls over my words, I add, "That doesn't mean I feel sorry for you. I wish you weren't in this situation."

I can tell she's both moved and troubled by my confession. I wish it was simpler, for both of us.

"You don't know me," she concludes with some regret, and maybe she has a point. That doesn't change the way I feel about her. I do want to know her.

"I know it sounds odd, and we've only met, but I care about you. This has taken me by surprise too, but it's not just about me. You deserve to be happy." To be desired. It could be so easy.

"Who says I'm not?"

"Don't you want more out of life?"

That, for some reason, makes her smile.

"I think you underestimate the value of friendship. We are not miserable. We can talk about everything."

"Except there's something he finds elsewhere."

Merin shrugs. "George is a good man. I'm not bitter or anything. We talked this through a long time ago, and now...This is our life, and it's not the worst. I can't give it up for a fantasy."

"I see. What if someone comes along who has more to offer than I do? You'll send them away too?"

I, too, am genuinely curious.

"I gave you all the answers I could give you." Merin stands, and I get to my feet as well. "Please, do me a favor and don't tell anyone."

"Because the truth is overrated? It sure seems that way in this town."

"Could you please just shut up?"

I didn't expect her to step into my personal space and kiss me, hungrily, but now that she's here I hold her to me, kiss her back with everything I failed to put into words. True, I have no idea what it's like, to have ties so strong to a particular place you'd make any compromise not to lose them. I had no idea this kind of thing still existed, and if it works for them, who am I to judge?

But Merin and George made choices based on a risk assessment in a toxic environment. No one, ever, should have to do that.

I'm of no help to anyone. I'm selfishly loving the feel of her in my arms, her mouth on mine.

Until the sound of a voice makes us both jump back.

"Aunt Merin, you're home, thank God!" Fiona sounds breathless. I look from her to Merin, the blush on her face. Fortunately, Fiona is too upset to notice. "Have you heard about Lucas? They say that Erica's dad shot him!"

"Who says that?" Merin asks before I can.

"I don't know, a lot of people in town. That's not right."

"Shooting him? No, that's not right," I agree. "He should be in jail instead of dead. Have you talked to Erica?"

She looks guilty. "No. I wouldn't know what to tell her. All of this sucks."

No kidding.

"Sit down for a second," Merin says. "You want a glass of iced tea?"

"Yes, please."

When Fiona and I are alone, I ask, "How are you doing?"

For a few seconds, her expression is blank, as if she doesn't know what I'm referring to.

"Oh, I'm okay. You heard they let Pete out, right? But he isn't going to try anything now that this has happened with Lucas. He's too worried he'll end up at the bottom of the lake as well."

Something about her words strikes me as odd, even though I agree with her. "Yeah. They're usually not that courageous."

Fiona scoffs. "No, they're not. But thank you for yesterday."

"No problem. If you don't mind me asking, have you thought about contacting Erica at all?"

"It's better to leave that alone," she says. Merin returns, and I'm aware it's my cue to leave.

I can't help wondering what other secrets lie beneath the surface, Fiona, her mother, the yet unidentified person who killed Lucas.

That person is still out there.

Is Erica in danger from them? She never wavered in her statement—she doesn't remember, and the case against Lucas was based on physical evidence.

But I've learned that in this town, everyone leaves out parts of the story.

Chapter Twelve

I take care of the most unpleasant part next, a brief stop at the Gavins' house.

"Don't worry, you'll get your money," Mr. Gavin tells me in a scathing tone. "You couldn't have waited until my son was in the earth, could you?"

I'm not sure if this is a display of grief, or more of his usual power play crap.

"I'm sorry for your loss," I say. "I just wanted to tell you in person."

"I'll send the check to the hotel. Now could you leave us alone?"

"Of course," I say, relieved when the door closes. I don't like it here at all, but this place, with the luxury and the hypocrisy it harbors, seems to be the worst of it.

I stop by the main street diner for a coffee and indulgence. The food is one of the few things that makes life here worth-while. As I expected, everyone's talking about Lucas Gavin's death, and within the first few minutes while I'm waiting for my order, I already hear a lot of theories floating around.

Mr. McQuade.

Drugs. A couple of co-workers from a nearby construction site wonder if Lucas was driven to a life of crime because of those accusations made, and they conclude that it's proof those radical feminists have gone too far.

I nearly laugh at that. I sure encountered a lot of radical ideas during my short stay. Feminist, not so much. My contempt for the gossiping townspeople only gets me so far before I think of Merin again. I'm well aware that my urge to—I don't know, free her? —isn't completely altruistic.

It bothers me that she has to hide who she is to keep a job and a roof over her head. Maybe it's because most of the time, those issues, those stories, are far away even for me. Being confronted with them is uncomfortable because there is no quick and easy fix. It makes me feel helpless. I don't do helpless. I am falling for her.

They made choices. Difficult ones, but they're not teens out on the streets because their parents rejected them. No one seems suicidal. They have an arrangement, and they made themselves as comfortable as they could be under the circumstances.

Perhaps the unknown is more frightening.

If only I had more to offer to her.

But the truth is, we barely know each other. I can't ask her to come with me and leave everything she knows behind.

I am falling. Failing.

The next moment, I am jolted out of my thoughts as my cup falls into my lap, hot coffee burning my thighs.

"What the hell?" I'm on my feet, more angry than hurt.

The man who pushed the cup off the table walks by whistling. Pete Bradley. The other patrons look on with interest, though some are probably more offended by my words than his act.

"Hey. Bradley! I'm talking to you."

He turns around and looks me up and down with a smirk.

"You just can't help yourself, can you? Making a scene wherever you go."

I'd love nothing more than give the spoiled brat a piece of my mind, but he's on the radar of local law enforcement. I want it to stay that way, not give him an easy out.

"Last time I checked you were the one getting arrested. I see Daddy posted bail."

He scoffs, about to walk away, but then he turns around and walks up close to me. I stand straight, looking him in the eye.

"You have something to say to me?"

"Look at you," he says with disdain. "This is not the town for a nosy bitch like you. Go back to where you came from."

I can't stand these entitled teenagers and their veiled threats.

"That's something we can agree on, I can't wait to go home. As for you...aren't you a bit more concerned about what happened to your buddy?"

"Oh, I am, very concerned." His smile says otherwise. "You're not threatening me, are you?"

Fed up with his antics, I leave him standing.

⌒⌒⌒

I would have liked to go straight to the hotel and change, but to my dismay, I run into someone familiar before I reach my car.

"Ms. Jameson, hi."

"Please, it's Kelli," I say awkwardly, and both George and I fall silent. Do I have to feel guilty for kissing his wife earlier today? For wanting her to leave him? He's been meeting another man for what seems to be a long period of time. Would he still be so friendly if he knew I knew?

"George," he says. "I assume your job here is now done? I'm sorry it ended on such a bad note."

"Thanks, George. I'll wrap up the report for my boss, and...yeah. After that, I guess I'm free to go." Unlike him. Or Merin. "I went to see Mr. Gavin earlier."

"They aren't the easiest neighbors to live with, but that must be horrible for them."

"Yeah."

He lingers, and before I can make my escape, he continues, "With everything that's been going on around here, it's not the best timing to think of a party, but we invited everyone already."

"A party?"

"Merin didn't tell you? It's her birthday tomorrow. Hey, why don't you come? You two seemed to have hit it off."

Either he didn't see me that night at the bar, or he's just cruel. A good man, Merin said.

"I don't know that it's a good idea. It's for your family, I imagine,"

"Family and some friends. You know Fiona. Like I said the other day, we don't want you to leave with the worst impression you could get of our hometown." He shakes his head. "Of course, that was before someone was killed. Please, come? Not all of us are bad."

"You and Merin have been very welcoming," I acknowledge. "I appreciate it."

"Good. I'll see you tomorrow at five?"

"You will."

I know it's a bad idea, but I can't seem to stay away either.
***

I finally go back to the hotel room to change, realizing that my skin is still reddened where the hot coffee hit it. I'll have to tough it out for now, since there's no ice anywhere here.

I'm not yet sure what to make of the encounter. There's nothing much Bradley can do, with the police already watching him. He's simply being obnoxious—and I doubt that even most of the patrons would take his side. He seems nervous. Perhaps I should find a way to talk to him again. If Erica's case was reopened...but that's just fantasy at this point. She and her family won't want to go through that again. Lucas is dead.

Except if there was another suspect...or suspects.

I can't stay here forever. People know my story, and they'd start to wonder if finding Lucas was really my incentive.

I refuse to be shaken by the encounter. He's an entitled spoiled brat who lied for his rapist friend.

Besides, now I have to find a present for Merin.

She's a teacher, so...a book? I find the one store in town, but the problem is I have no idea what kind of books she prefers. She teaches history, so she has an interest there, but maybe she likes to take a break from it when she reads for pleasure?

I should have asked George, her long-time friend, the good man. He's bound to know her tastes, and for some reason that makes me petty and jealous. What is he giving her for her birthday? Jewelry? I leave the bookstore and walk past other buildings on main street, a realtor, the office of an insurance company.

A jeweler.

How petty and jealous am I really? I've known her for a few days. I'm attracted to her, and while she seems to feel the same, Merin has never had a relationship with a woman, or at least that's what I caught between the lines. She might want to, but that would mean giving up everything she knows. You can't ask that of anyone unless they're ready to do it. It would make me no better than the people in town who force their lifestyle on their neighbors.

With a sigh, I walk past the jeweler, then come back and look at the bracelets in the window. A bracelet. You can give that to a friend, can't you? A thought is forming, and it might be irrational, a fantasy, but it's the best I can do for now.

The moon pendant reminds me of the night we sat outside, talking, when all the complications weren't yet out in the open, only possibilities. I want her to know that if she changes her mind, she can always rely on me. It's not contingent on anything. If she wants to leave this place and start over somewhere else, I'll help her any way I can. Take her somewhere she could meet someone...Okay, I'm getting far ahead of myself. Merin is an adult, capable, someone who has already made her choices.

I want her to know that there are always options, especially when her current arrangement isn't equal.

I walk inside the store and buy the bracelet. On my way back, I buy a book from the table right by the entrance of the bookstore, a recent bestseller, a historical mystery. That's inconspicuous enough in case I lose my courage.

With a little luck, I'll be able to leave town after the party.

My last stop of the day is at the police station. Cross is not available, but Officer Woodward is behind the front desk.

"The sheriff is busy right now," she says. "He's meeting with a homicide detective from the county."

"I was wondering if there is any news regarding the murder weapon. Sheriff Cross told me he needed to take a look at my gun to rule it out, but I haven't heard from him. I'd like to leave town as soon as possible, given the weather forecast."

Her eyes widen momentarily, then she nods. "Let's hope it won't be too bad. We had a lot of destruction a couple of years ago."

"My gun?" I remind her.

"I'm surprised he didn't call you. It was a hunting rifle. You didn't bring one of those, did you?"

"No, Officer."

"Wait a second. I'll let him know you're here."

She picks up the phone and gives me a pointed look, so I step back and give her some privacy. The conversation is short and fairly one-sided. Liz Woodward makes another quick call, and a couple of minutes later, another officer arrives with my gun. She takes it from him and hands it to me.

"There you go. I just need your signature here."

At least something is going smoothly. I sign and push the paper back to her.

"Have a good day, Ms. Jameson."

"Thank you," I reply and leave, lost in thought.

Why indeed didn't he tell me? And what does that mean? I assume that a few people in town have these kinds of rifles.

Does Mr. McQuade? Or one of Lucas's buddies, who didn't want him to tell the whole truth if it conflicted with his earlier version?

In the hotel room, I slip the small box containing the bracelet into the giftbag with the book and put it in my suitcase for now. If I'm so fed up with people's lack of courage, their penchant to bend the truth, how do I measure up? Only one way to find out, tomorrow night, at Merin's birthday party.

I call Pete Bradley, and to my surprise, he picks up.

"What the hell do you want?"

"Just talk. You know I'm going to leave soon, but my boss is friends with Lucas's parents, and I'll have to tell him something. You owe me a coffee."

"Really? You nearly shot me. Wouldn't surprise me if you killed Lucas."

"I didn't. And you shouldn't be threatening young girls in the forest, but here we are. Just meet me for a beer in the bar on Main Street. You pay, and I'll leave you alone."

"What if I say no?"

I push a bit further. "All this time I was thinking Lucas might have a prior record, something that was tied to his disappearance. Now I wonder if it's not one of his friends."

"You've got to ask Kyle. He was there."

"I'm asking you."

"All right," he relents. "I'll be there in an hour. No bullshit."

That's rich coming from him, but I don't bring it up. I'll keep my ears and eyes open one last time. See Merin tomorrow, one last time.

I still hate this case, because it throws everything that's wrong with the world back in my face—and I can't do a damn thing about it.

He's late. That doesn't surprise me. I'm surprised that he shows up at all. Pete doesn't seem to worry about being seen with me after the scene in the diner either, because he stops at the bar to chat with the bartender before he joins me at the table.

"All right Ma'am. You had questions. Ask them, I don't have all night."

That is on purpose too. Sometimes, with everything disgusting they do and say, I forget how young they are. But that means nothing. These young men were brought up to believe that they are owed by others, and that they can just take whatever they want. It's not their fault that they were given these lessons as children.

It's absolutely their fault that they refuse to challenge them as adults. Affluenza. It's real.

"Fair enough. What did you mean when you told Fiona that what happened to Erica could happen to her?"

He stares back at me, unimpressed. "Why are you even still here? They found Lucas. End of story."

"Oh, but the story is just beginning, because someone put a bullet in his chest. You haven't answered my question."

"Just a figure of speech," he says. "Everyone's been talking about her for months. Fiona tells the same lies, that's what will happen to her. That's it."

"You mean you weren't threatening her with rape."

"No one raped anyone," he says, trying his best to look bored. "Lucas and Erica hooked up at the party. The next day, she had regrets. That's it."

"Except someone didn't believe it. And they made their point with a rifle."

"Yeah, maybe, but they were wrong. We got drunk, okay? That's all that happened. Do you have any other questions?"

"You do that often, get drunk at parties? Are there any drugs involved?"

We both know I know the answer to that question already. It would be naïve to assume otherwise. He's cautious.

"I'm not going to tell the cops about what you drank or smoked. That's not the point here."

"Someone brings pot sometimes," he admits.

"Who? Lucas?"

"No, not him. It was only a couple of times, and nothing other than that."

If there had been, he probably wouldn't admit it.

"Kyle told me he talked to Lucas a few days before he disappeared, that everything was normal. Did you have the same impression when you last heard from him?"

"Yes. He was trying to get on with life, all right?"

"He didn't mention anyone threatening him? Think carefully. The same person, or people, might come after you."

He laughs at that. "Let them try. I hunt too."

"So, you have no idea who could have killed Lucas. Why were you meeting Fiona in the woods? Was she Lucas's girlfriend?"

He sits up a bit straighter, and I know I'm on to something. That would explain why the girls distanced themselves from Erica. Merin will not be happy.

"He didn't have a girlfriend as far as I know. He was always hooking up with girls at parties."

Classy.

"Fiona?"

"She wanted to talk to me, but I told her the same thing. I don't know anything about what happened with Lucas. He didn't do anything wrong except drink too much. "

"And you're not worried at all?"

"You keep saying that. You know something I don't?"

"Not really," I say and get up. "Thanks for the beer."

He doesn't protest, and that is surprising too.

Back at the hotel, I see that my mother called. I call her back, and her first question is, "How's Hawaii? I hope you're relaxing?"

"I am. I said I'd call you once I'm home. What's going on?"

"Oh, I just wanted to know if you're coming home for Thanksgiving. I know you're busy, but it would be nice to be together for a bit..."

I hear the unspoken question. No, it's not likely that I'll bring anyone.

"Yes, I agree. I'll try to make it. Is everything okay?"

"Oh yes. We're completely booked."

My parents, too, can be a bit sentimental about small-town living, though my mom's hometown, where they bought a bed & breakfast three years ago, is close enough to the city for my comfort. Romantic, by the coast. They put a small rainbow flag in the window as well. People don't come to hide away.

I'm far, far from home, and I can't deal with any distractions now.

"That's great. I will call you when I'm back."

I end the call before she can ask any more questions, or I'd have to face the lies I told to people that matter to me. Not now.

Chapter Thirteen

I didn't think I'd go to any party during my stay here, which means my wardrobe isn't exactly fitting. I'll stand out as it is, but since everyone's still suffering from the heat, and it's the afternoon, a light pair of pants and the black sleeveless top will do. I hope. There are six cars parked in front. George is out the door before I even have the chance to exit my car and greets me at the bottom of the front steps.

I have the impulse to run, but instead I shake his hand.

"Thanks for inviting me." Along with the gift, I brought a bottle of wine.

"Thank you so much for coming. Everyone's out in the back-yard."

I follow him inside the house, where he puts the wine in the fridge and my gift bag on a table with an already impressive number of presents. "Would you like something to drink?"

I have to be careful since I'll be driving back, but I'm not sure I can make it through this evening stone cold sober.

"A beer would be great," I say, and that moment, Merin appears. I can tell right away that she didn't expect me here. Damn it, George.

"Surprise," he says good-naturedly.

Merin catches herself and smiles. "It's a nice one. Welcome, Kelli."

"Thanks for having me. Happy birthday."

I'm not sure how to interpret her expression. It's gone in a flash, and the smile is back.

"Come with me," she says. "The snacks are outside."

"I can't wait."

That's a lie, and we both know it. About two dozen people are crowding the backyard, chatting, drinking. I realize that some of them are vaguely familiar, people I've seen around town. Fiona and her parents are here too. I would have been able to blend in if it was just about clothes, but I'm still the suspicious newcomer.

At the buffet, she asks me, "Why are you here again?"

I was afraid this would happen. "I suppose I'm the surprise guest."

"Did you say anything to George?"

"It's not my place," I say, offended that she could think this of me. "Look, I'm sorry. I'll find an excuse to leave soon."

"I didn't know you were friends with Ms. Jameson." I don't need to be introduced to the older woman.

"You know now," Merin mumbles. "She'll be home in a few days. We're trying to give her a better impression of our town."

"I don't know why anyone would get a bad impression other than what's been said on the Internet, from people who don't know us. Tragedies can happen anywhere."

"They do," I agree. "Nice to meet you. Merin and George have a beautiful home here."

Why do I have to say this every time? Merin sends me a stormy look. "Mom, didn't you want George to help you with something?"

"Oh, right. We'll talk later, dear."

I am about to apologize again, but a woman of Merin's age, someone I haven't met before, comes by. She gives me a curious look. "Merin, we need you over here."

"Excuse me for a moment?" she asks, sounding frustrated. Before being whisked away, the woman reaches out a hand.

"I'm Caitlyn, Merin's friend."

"Hi. I'm Kelli."

There's a moment of undeniable tension before they leave me at the buffet. While I'm here, I might as well take advantage.

"That's a surprise, seeing you here."

I turn around, coming face to face with someone I only met briefly before, Fiona's mom. I'm not sure if that emotion coming through in her voice is frustration or anger, or why she would be angry at me.

"It's a small world. How is Fiona doing?"

"She's doing okay. She'd be better if she wasn't sneaking around in the woods at night, alone."

"She should be able to go wherever she wants to go, without being attacked," I argue. "Same goes for Erica, or anyone else."

Whoa, I need to slow down on the beer, or I'll have to walk home.

"I agree. And I think you might have gotten the wrong idea."

"How so?"

"I know you've been asking around about the girls, and why they stopped seeing Erica," Ellen explains. "A lot of people have opinions on that. I never told Fiona to stop being friends with Erica."

"What is your opinion on what happened, then?"

I notice that she looks tired. Then again, we all are. Perhaps cooler temperatures would help, though they wouldn't fix everything that's wrong around here.

"Honestly? I don't know. I think this whole thing has shaken them. No one wants to believe this could happen to them."

"That doesn't make the underlying problem go away though, does it?"

"I don't know what to tell you."

"Merin told me you work for the Gavins' company. That family seems to have an unsettling amount of power around here."

She seems almost amused at that.

"Rich people don't have a lot of power where you come from? I find that hard to believe."

Unfortunately, she has a point.

"Did you talk to Fiona about why she was meeting Pete Bradley?"

She shakes her head. "You're wrong on this too. She wasn't meeting him. She was just taking a walk."

At night, in the woods?

The police have looked at the area because it's close to the lake where they found Lucas, but it won't hurt to take a second look. I have a feeling that I won't stay long tonight anyway.

"Yeah, I must have been mistaken. I'm sorry."

"We try our best to protect the people we love. It isn't always easy."

I can relate. I'd love to get her sister out of here.

But like so many things, it's not up to me.

❧

When I go inside in search of another beer Merin steps into my path.

"Come with me," she says.

I don't ask, just follow her further into the house and into—wow. That's the main suite.

"I could kill him," she says with startling anger. "Yes, I know, bad choice of words. Why did he have to do that? Why did you say yes?"

"Because I thought it was understood that we'd pretend nothing ever happened. Merin. I get it. You made your choices.

I had no right to question any of them." It pains me to say it. That doesn't make it any less true. "I'll soon be gone, but I wanted you to know something. If you ever want to talk, or just a time-out from all of this, you can call me. Come visit me if you like. No strings attached. I promise."

She sits on the side of the bed, holding her head in her hands for a moment before she looks back up at me.

"A few weeks ago, I couldn't even imagine...Yes, of course it was all horrible, but this had nothing to do with any of it. This is our home! It's Erica's home too. What if everyone just ran away?"

"They haven't been treating Erica the way they should. And everything tells me that if you or George ever came out, they'd be just as awful to you. I understand that not everyone has the means to leave. But that's not the case for you two."

She looks at me in disbelief. Perhaps there's something I still don't understand.

"How can I ask anyone to accept me if I don't even know who I am?"

So much pain for no reason. I don't know if I want to cry, or punch somebody. Who says that violence doesn't solve problems? Lucas will never hurt another girl. That's not a bad outcome in my book. I push those dark thoughts aside and sit next to her on the bed.

"You need a moment, that's understandable. It will all make sense, but there's no reason for anyone not to accept you while you're figuring it out."

"It sounds so easy when you say it," she says with a sigh.

"It is. Just don't kill George. He really meant well."

Despite herself, she starts laughing, and I'm a little proud of myself. Too hopeful.

"Yeah, he always does." Merin's tone is sober now. "He's kind, and so I can't really be mad at him, can I? Because that would be petty. But I am mad sometimes. We made a promise in front of our families. If I could keep it, why couldn't he?"

I take her hand, holding it in mine. She doesn't pull back.

For once, I know when to shut up. I don't need to ask the hard questions—she's known the answers for some time. Because he's not attracted to her, not that way. Because he is looking for more than their comfortable platonic arrangement, and because of that, they aren't on the same page any longer.

She leans into me, and I put my arms around her.

"I meant it. You can always call me."

"Thank you." She straightens, regret in her gaze. "Things have been crazy around here ever since Lucas was charged. I believe it will all calm down at some point. Erica is getting help."

Will it be enough? I don't have an answer for the implied question.

"You can always change your mind, you know."

"The school needs me. The girls need me. I would lose everything for—what?"

"Your chance to live an authentic life. Somewhere, with someone who can't imagine living without you."

I wish that could be me. We all have our illusions.

"It's too late for that."

"It's never too late."

"It is for Lucas to come forward and do something decent in his life, don't you think? I need to go downstairs. They must be wondering where I am." She gets up and walks to the door, turning to cast me an impatient look when I don't move. "What?"

"You asked me to come here. What was it you wanted to tell me?"

"I'm sorry," she says after a long pause. "I'm really sorry." Her eyes fill with tears.

"Don't be. Nothing happened."

"But I wanted it to. And it's not fair of me to use you that way, just because I'm confused and jealous. Maybe George and I could get counseling." That fledgling hope in her voice is heartbreaking.

"If you want to stay married, maybe, but counseling won't make either of you straight."

"Could you stop throwing the truth in my face?"

She's frustrated. So am I, and this is getting us nowhere. I get up and walk over to her. "I should go. I wish you all the best, Merin." I hold her hand for a brief moment before I reach for the door handle.

"Wait. Please. Can we meet somewhere tomorrow, just talk?"

I can't back out now. I promised.

"Yes, of course. I have an idea where we can go."

Chapter Fourteen

I don't stay for the cake or the gifts. I'm sure I'll be able to explain tomorrow. There's still something in the air, something worse than Merin's complex situation. Lucas Gavin was murdered, and it doesn't seem like the police have any idea who did it. What if it wasn't related to the rape at all? What if everyone in this town is in danger from the person who did it?

Am I melodramatic? Paranoid? The boss sent me here for a reason. I overreacted—his words, not mine—and he wanted to teach me a lesson. Aside from that, he knows I'm stubborn, and I'm good at my job. Something feels very wrong, beyond people throwing money and power around, beyond the ones who took Lucas's side, beyond bigotry.

There's more to the story.

I might not be able to unravel it all. Unfinished business. In my opinion, that's worse than crossing a line.

I'm jolted out of my thoughts when I see the lights flash and realize that I'm being pulled over. I have no idea why. We're alone on a long stretch of road, and there's nothing wrong with my driving. My license plate is up to date. What is their problem?

I park on the side of the road and lower the window.

The officer walks up to me.

"Good evening." I've seen him a couple of times at the station. "Is anything wrong?"

"License and registration, please, Ma'am."

"What's the matter? I was visiting the Burkes. You know who I am, right?" Calm down, Kelli. That's probably not what he's interested in. I hand him the papers, and he studies them with a frown.

"Step out of the car."

They've got to be kidding me.

"Excuse me?"

"Now!"

Perplexed, angry, and a alarmed, I open the door and step outside, wincing when he pushes me up against the side of the car. Another officer comes up behind us. I recognize LeBlanc.

"This must be a misunderstanding," I say. "I was just visiting a friend."

"Please, Ms. Jameson, stay calm," Officer LeBlanc tells me. He peers into the car.

"Keep your hands on the roof," his colleague instructs.

"Sure. Could you tell me what you are looking for?"

"Whatever it is *you* are looking for, you should stop," he sneers while LeBlanc looks on, seeming bored. "You were lurking in the woods the other day where Lucas Gavin was found. Now Pete Bradley says you threatened him. You leave him alone."

"I didn't do anything...If he says otherwise, he's lying..."

He pushes me hard enough for me to stumble to my knees.

"Don't make things worse for yourself or anyone around here," he warns. They both walk back to their car and drive away. I struggle to my feet and back into the driver's seat. Only after I've locked the door, I realize I'm shaking hard, my teeth nearly chattering even though it's still hot and humid.

What the hell was that?

I make it back to the hotel room after making a quick stop at a gas station to buy a six pack. In my room, I open the first bottle and take a long swallow, and another. Eventually, the feeling of utter dread vanishes, making room for rage.

The police too. Not that it surprises me. Sheriff Cross seemed reluctant whenever it came to holding one of the "good boys" accountable. I can't believe those officers would undertake an effort like this without his go-ahead.

What were they thinking? Are they on the Gavins' payroll—and maybe the Bradleys'? Where does it end? I don't think anyone will make a serious attempt to pin Lucas's death on me, but the message is pretty clear: They want me to stop looking. Get lost. Maybe I should.

I thought there was nothing left here for me, but if they try so hard to keep me from investigating, what does that mean? Just a display of power, or more?

I rake a hand through my hair, put down the bottle, pick it up again. I'm halfway through the second when I allow myself to think of Merin again. I wish I could help her, be the better friend she needs right now, not a woman with a fantasy of her own.

She's conflicted, which is easy to understand. It's just so foreign from my own experience, and frankly, I don't think anyone should go through what she is going through. All this angst because of people who think of themselves as good and righteous, unwilling to understand that in fact they are acting selfish and doing harm to the ones they pretend to care about.

Even George.

What he's doing looks like it's stretching the boundaries of their agreement. Or it's possible that they failed to re-negotiate those boundaries once it became necessary. A lavender marriage. The last time I heard that term was a long time ago, reading for some undergrad studies...I didn't even realize this kind of thing existed in the present. And don't get me wrong, straight people get married for all kinds of dubious reasons. If they are truly happy with it, who cares?

But George goes out of town to date, and Merin? I'm not sure what it's like for her, except that she has a lot of unexplored feelings. There's little chance she's going to explore them with me.

I'm going around in cycles. Sometime later that night, I'm reminded of the promise I made to her.

Should I, still?

Is it safe for her, or for me?

Is it selfish?

I was just threatened by a couple of police officers. I think I have earned the right to be a little selfish.

Speaking to my mother seems like forever ago, but remembering the call, I wish I could drop everything and go now.

I wish I could take Merin with me, escape the dreadful heat and make love to the sound of the ocean. That might be the alcohol speaking, but I can see it all so clearly.

***

After a hearty breakfast, I've decided I'm not going to let a couple of small-town bullies intimidate me, even if they wear a uniform. What are they going to do? My boss would intervene if they wanted to frame me for a murder that happened before I had even heard of this town.

I drive back to the clearing where I saw Pete and Fiona, park my car so it's hidden by tall bushes, and venture further into the forest. It's not a huge area, so I'm not in any danger of getting lost. After a few minutes, the path leads to a higher area from which I can see the lake. It occurs to me that Lucas might have been killed in these woods.

Fiona might have lied to her mother, but if she thought Pete had something to do with the murder, why would she meet him alone? Given the history he and his buddies had?

A piece of plastic catches on my heel, and I realize it's a piece of yellow tape. Danger. Did the sheriff and his team find the crime scene? I walk the path all the way to its end to come up to a wooden shack, a part of it hidden by low-hanging branches. All the windows are broken, and the front door is off its hinges.

Why would teenagers of the town hang out around here anyway? A dare? I know you're supposed to do something that scares you, every day, but I'm pretty sure it doesn't mean you should risk getting yourself killed.

Like I'm doing now, walking over the threshold of the place that looks like it's about to fall on me. Did Lucas come here as well, to meet someone? The person who shot him and dumped his body in the lake below?

The inside is more spacious than it looked from outside. The remains of a kitchen counter, a cabinet about to lose its fight with gravity. Some furniture. A rocking chair in a corner, a sofa partly covered in dust.

Partly. I can see footsteps on the floor. Several people have been in here, recently, police, I assume. Even though I know they've searched the space, I want to take a look myself. This place is too creepy not to be relevant. If I had a black light available, I'm sure it would light up. As it is, it's pretty dark in here, not much sunlight making it past the trees.

In a corner, close to the window, I find it, a smear of...something, and then more pale stains on the floor. I bet that Lucas was shot in this space. Someone tried to clean up afterwards, with moderate success. Turning away, I walk to the other side of the room. I reach out, think twice, and use a tissue to open the door. I'm more concerned about health hazards than I am about leaving fingerprints, though given what happened yesterday, I should wipe the handle on the way out as well. Just to be on the safe side.

The bathroom is in the condition I expected it to be in. It smells bad. I step inside anyway, determined—to make it quick, mostly. I take a look around, and at the floor. Broken tiles, a toilet...No deep breaths, I remind myself. Underneath it, I see something glinting. Using the same tissue, wincing a few more times, I reach out and pick it up. It's an earring. It looks a lot like the jewelry I saw in the store where I bought Merin's gift. I wrap it in tissue paper and put it in the pocket of my jeans when I hear the sound.

Yeah, maybe I'm the reckless one, sneaking around a crime scene after the local police warned me to stay away in not so polite terms. Keeping ears and eyes open, right? I paid my dues, and then a lot more.

There is no back door. I cautiously make my way to the front door, keeping my head down, staying away from the windows. Ironic that my boss told me to do just that, though I assume he was talking about tornadoes. I could still make it out without seeing one, though the forecast's warnings are becoming even more dire. Severe thunderstorms, flooding, possible tornadoes. I don't want to be driving to the airport when one of them hits.

Another sound tells me that someone is on the other side of that door.

I put my hand on my gun, and with the other, I yank the door open to reveal Lexi Adams.

After a few seconds of startled silence from both of us, I say, "You shouldn't be here."

"Look who's talking," she snaps.

"I'm serious. It appears that Lucas was killed here. There's blood on the floor."

"Could be anything," she says. "People get hurt."

"People in general?" I ask as we walk back to the path. "Or do you mean someone specific? What *were* you doing here?"

"You're not the police, are you? Technically, I don't have to answer any of your questions."

"Technically, that's true." I shrug. "But I'm here, and you're here. That means we probably have some of the same questions, and one of them is who killed Lucas. Maybe there's a way we could help each other."

"I don't see how."

I'm alarmed when all of a sudden, she starts to cry.

"Lexi. Are you okay?" I pray it's nothing that requires involving the local authorities. I've been on the fence before, but now I'm sure that I can't trust them. I'm surprised they didn't find the earring though. Coincidence? Another cover-up?

"No, I'm not. I hate this."

"Would you like to go and get a snack somewhere? Talk?"

She shakes her head and wipes her face. "Thanks, but no. I kinda don't want to be seen with you."

"Fair enough. It's been pretty taxing for all of you."

"I don't know, maybe we should have supported Erica more."

I absolutely agree with that.

"You were friends. What happened?"

Will one of them finally be honest? Did Fiona date Pete?

"I'm not even sure."

"Did Fiona talk to you about what happened here in the woods a couple of days ago? What he said to her?"

She nods. "You saved her...and then you went to have a beer with him afterwards."

"All I want is to find the truth."

"Because it will set you free?" Her tone reveals her doubts.

"Because it's my job. It's not too late, you know. You can still reach out to Erica." It's only for Erica's benefit that I'm pushing the issue. An apology from the girls could be helpful.

"You think the police still suspect her dad?" Lexi asks.

"I don't know. Does he hunt? I've been told Pete Bradley does."

She shudders. "Mr. and Mrs. McQuade were always so nice to us. But we had no choice. People would have said we're just making things up because we're friends with her. We wanted them to hear the story from her, to know the truth."

"But they didn't believe the truth."

I'm not sure if what she says makes any sense to me. Wouldn't the first impulse be to support a friend no matter what anyone said? Unless someone held something over them.

"Pete is friends with some of the officers in town?"

"That has nothing to do with anything." She catches on quickly.

"Doesn't it? I was stopped on the road last night. The message went something like this, leave poor little Pete alone."

"I can imagine," she scoffs. "Well, you won't have to worry about them."

"Why is that?"

"You'll be going home, right? We can take care of ourselves."

"Lexi, it doesn't stop with the sheriff, whatever he says. There are people he and his folks have to answer to."

She studies me for a moment, as if to gauge what to tell me.

"Like I said, you don't have anything to worry about."

"I might be able to help."

"We're good. Thanks for the pep talk, Ms. Jameson. I don't need a ride."

Chapter Fifteen

A side from my more or less transparent intentions, I need Merin. She doesn't know all the facts, but she knows the people in this town, the girls in her class. Her perspective is invaluable to me, especially with the new developments. That's why I plan on taking her out tonight.

"I promised you something," I tell her after she picks up the phone. "Trust me?"

On the other end, Merin laughs. "Do I have a choice?"

"No, not really. I want us to go out tonight, talk, maybe even have a little fun. No one has earned it more than you. You think you could do an overnight stay?"

It takes a few seconds of silence before I realize how that might sound. "Okay, let me rephrase. I don't plan on kidnapping you, and you can have your own bed, or room, even."

"That sounds...elaborate," she comments. She doesn't say no.

"It's probably the last time before I leave. Please."

"Okay," she says. "You don't have to pay for anything though. You went above and beyond with the gift."

"The historical mystery? Yeah, I thought that was really imaginative."

"Kelli."

"Take it as a symbol. If you need to get out of town, call me. That's all."

"I need to talk to George," she says, her voice sounding small all of a sudden.

"Because you want to spend a day out of town with a friend? I don't see why he would object to that."

"No...in general. I just need to make sure I know where we stand, that we're still in this together." She sighs. "I did my best not to think about it, but...He's been seeing this guy for a while. I'm not sure what it means, for him, for me, but I need to find out eventually."

"I agree. It will serve both of you."

"I hope you're right. Okay. Let's go out. So, will you surprise me? What do I wear?"

"Casual. Just to relax, have a drink or two. I'll take you to a fancy restaurant when you come visit me on the East Coast."

I wonder if I've gone too far making it sound like a done deal. If that bothers Merin, she doesn't mention it.

"I can do casual," she says. "You're going to pick me up?"

"Around five-thirty. We'll have a bit of a drive ahead of us."

Before that, I have another errand to run.

❦

The jeweler remembers me, which is not a surprise. By now, I assume everyone in town knows who I am, for better or worse.

"Can I show you something else?" she asks.

"Actually, I wanted to show *you* something. I found this...and I'm not sure if it's worth a lot, or who lost it. But if it belongs to someone from around town, they might have bought it here."

"There's a good chance. Let me see?"

In another life, I would have brought this to the police and have them do an analysis. As it is, I think it's smarter not to involve Cross, LeBlanc, and the others. I cleaned the earring with water and soap, aware I probably erased evidence. Call it a hunch.

The jeweler takes a closer look.

"You recognize this earring?"

"Yes. This is silver. I made these and others last year. Where did you find it?"

"In town," I say vaguely. "Could you tell me who bought it? I'd like to return it."

I can sense her hesitation.

"I'm not sure I should give you that information. As a private investigator, do you have something like a warrant?"

I knew it.

"Not really," I admit, "but it's not like someone committed a crime. I picked this up from the floor, and it's probably meaningful to the person who bought it. I don't need their credit card information," I joke. "You just give me a name, and I can figure out the rest."

"Well, I think you know her. Merin bought them last Christmas."

"What a coincidence, yes, I do know her." I give her a polite smile, barely able to hide my inner turmoil. What does that mean? Was she in that shack, the night Lucas died, or on another occasion?

Did Merin have a motive?

Tonight might not be the relaxed outing I had in mind.

⁂

Nevertheless, I get ready for a night out on the town, and by the time I knock on the front door, I have talked myself into considering scenarios that are slightly less alarming. Merin bought the earrings around Christmas. She might have given them to someone as a gift. It's a lot more likely that they belong to Fiona, given that I ran into Lexi at the shack.

Well, that opens up another world of alarming scenarios, but I'm selfish enough to wish anyone but Merin lost that earring in a disgusting, dilapidated bathroom in the woods.

George opens the door to me with a welcoming smile. I'm not sure if I want to return it or shake him for...I don't really have much of a reason other than my pettiness. I don't know if he's been stringing Merin along, making her think that maybe someday, he might desire her—or did she know all along that they'd never have that kind of relationship?

"Come on in. Merin is almost ready. Can I offer you something?"

"No thanks. I'll just wait."

"Thank you for this," he says. "We've been so busy with...everything. Merin deserves a time-out, but she always thinks of others first."

"It's just dinner," I remind him. "But she definitely deserves it."

"I'm glad you think so."

He doesn't comment on that but casts a glance towards the stairs. Still no sign of Merin. Does he suspect that I know? Did she tell him? I'm not sure he'd still be this polite, then again, they've been living like this for a long time. My opinion isn't all that important here. Finally, a door opens, and Merin appears on top of the stairs.

I might have gasped, but compose myself quickly, as I realize that George is studying me, not her.

I still think this might be a good idea. I don't have a lot of illusions. The unknown seems to scare them more than anything, more than the devil they know, their "friendly" neighbors that wouldn't hesitate to turn on them at any moment.

I won't change that. But I want to show Merin that if George has alternatives, so does she. It's not about me. There's not going to be a happy ending.

Just a moment in time.

"You look amazing," I say, and I mean every word of it. A bit overdressed for where we're going, maybe, but that doesn't matter. We'll have a break from this place for one night.

"You girls have fun," George says. I listen carefully for any hidden meaning, not finding any.

"Thanks. See you tomorrow."

Merin looks thoughtful. When she realizes that I'm waiting for her, she kisses George on the cheek. "Good night. Don't do anything I wouldn't do."

That, right there, might have a hidden meaning. I have to admit I'm clueless as to how a relationship like theirs can work.

"That's good advice. Let's go."

"Where are we going?" Merin asks when we are in the car.

"You still trust me?"

"It's not a matter of trust."

"It's a surprise." I notice she's wearing the bracelet. "You like it?"

"Yes. I found it hidden in the gift bag of the book you gave me. What a coincidence, right?"

We share a smile. Hers makes me all too warm and tingly inside. I have to concentrate on driving.

"I don't want you to get the wrong idea," I start.

"I won't. I know that all of this is hard to understand. To be honest? I'm questioning myself a lot, but then I try not to. I know the girls need me, and my family needs me. I could do a lot worse than George."

She could also do a lot better. I don't argue. That might look like sour grapes.

"I actually did grow up in a small town," I say. "No one bullied me, but I didn't love it either."

"Why did you leave?" she asks, genuinely curious.

"Not enough options. I needed to see what else was out there." It's been a good enough explanation all these years, though in the present, I wonder how far it's gotten me. Working for a boss who assigned me to what was, at least partly, a private errand. Single, fantasizing about a married woman.

But I don't hide who I am, from anyone.

With small, necessary exceptions. It's a bit of a vicious cycle.

"And, did you? Find something different, better?"

"I'm here now, chasing ghosts. You tell me."

She leans back in her seat, looking ahead. "I know the circumstances weren't the best. They're horrible, in fact. But I'm glad we met."

"Because of that historical mystery I gave you?"

"That, too," she says, laughing. "Now where's that place? I'm hungry."

"Don't worry. We'll be there in a few minutes."

"Are you kidding me?"

Not much later, I realize the evening isn't going as well as I hoped it would. Perhaps I did get ahead of myself. But I still think my intentions are valid.

"Hear me out, please?"

Merin looks around, her disapproval written all over her face. "You know that this is the place where George goes."

"Not tonight, though. I'll admit it's tricky, but there aren't so many choices in the vicinity. I wanted to spend an evening out with you in a safe space, that's all."

"You're sure you didn't want to rub it in? How I'm missing out?"

She's serious, and I realize I only have a small window of opportunity here before she'll ask me to drive her home.

"No, that was never my intention. We said we'd talk, well, no one will bother us here. They do have pretty good food and drinks." Last resort. "Please, don't be mad at me?"

Merin sighs. "I guess I can either forgive you, or I'd have to make a scene and demand you drive all the way back...Frankly, I'm too hungry for the latter. So, bring it, what food is so great that we had to come here?"

"Let's go in and take a look at the menu," I say, relieved. For a moment, my fantasy was teetering on the edge. I can get it back on track.

When we walk inside, the blue-haired bartender recognizes me and waves. The other patrons go about their business, talk, laugh, eat, and drink in a place where nobody's giving them strange looks. This is what I wanted her to experience above else. But yes, the food too. We order a burger each and a side of fries to share, with a couple of beers.

After the first sip, she leans back in her chair, her gaze on me somewhere between curious and amused.

"What?"

"I'm still trying to figure you out. Your motivation for this. You've said I don't owe you anything, but the same is true vice versa."

"Sure," I say with a shrug. "Maybe I wanted something good to come out of this chaos."

"Well, you didn't promise too much on the food and drinks."

"It's a start."

It's irrational, me, taking her to a bar like we're on a date. But we're both good at pretending, so it works in some way.

"I'm not trying to lure you away from everything you know," I clarify. "This is just one night."

"I get it."

"Don't you get tired of looking over your shoulder? With a handful of families controlling everything in this town?"

"Sure, sometimes," Merin admits. "I appreciate this, and everything you offered. But being a lesbian isn't all I am."

Between the two of us, it's still unclear who's the one not getting it.

"The same is true for me."

"At home, at work, does everyone know?"

"Pretty much. If someone can't stand to be around me, it's because of my personality, I guess."

"I think your personality is just fine." She reaches for her glass again. "Thank you, Kelli."

I'm not sure I follow.

"I mean it. Aside from the occasional dinner party, we go to the diner and the bar in town. I keep thinking that's how female teachers in the early nineteen-hundreds must have felt, when they weren't allowed to be seen in public. That's not because of our...situation. We both work hard."

"I understand." At least I'm trying to. We both take a sip of our beer.

"We were talking about taking a vacation, but that seems like forever ago," she continues. "The timing is never right. We both built a career here. We can't give that up just because some people don't agree with who we are."

People who "don't agree" with the existence of others give me a headache. But I don't want to have that conversation now.

"You shouldn't have to," I say instead. "I agree. Let's play a game. If you could go tomorrow, where would you like to go?"

"San Francisco," she says without hesitation, and laughs. "Does that sound like too much of a cliché? George has a brother there, and I've seen some pictures. It's beautiful."

"You like the sea?"

"I love it. We once rented a condo in Myrtle Beach."

"My parents live by the coast. They own a Bed & Breakfast. When you come visit me, we could spend a few days there."

I'm in over my head.

"So, it's already decided." I knew I couldn't sneak that past her.

"What do you think?"

"That would be great," she says, her voice full of longing. I have a hard time not getting distracted. This is what she needs, a time-out, a vacation maybe...a friend. This is what I signed up for. Nothing more.

"Whenever you want to give it a try, I'll make time," I promise.

Chapter Sixteen

I have proof that Merin does trust me. As the night proceeds, we make it to the small dance floor. We have a couple of cocktails. At about 1:40 a.m., we retreat to our room. I found a little hotel tucked away from the main road—even if we come here as friends, I decided the motel was a tad too tacky. I spring for a cab, too.

"What about your car?"

"I'll get it tomorrow. It will survive a night in the parking lot."

It's the last thing on my mind.

The hotel room has two double beds. I sit on mine as I wait for my turn in the bathroom.

She's wearing a tank top and shorts when she returns, her hair still slightly damp. I get to my feet abruptly. Friends, I remind myself.

After one quick, tepid shower, I crawl under my own covers, thinking she's asleep, until she speaks.

"I'm glad we did this," she says. "It was unreal, but good."

"I'm glad too."

"I still can't forget about Lucas. I know he did something horrible, but I can't be happy he'd dead."

I sit up in bed and turn on the light on my side. We face each other.

"A violent death is hardly something to be happy about."

"For sure, he can't hurt anyone else, but I wish there had been another way to achieve that. I wish he had realized what he'd done." Her conflicted emotions are visible on her face. I want nothing more than hug her close, but it's important she doesn't misunderstand my intentions. It's important I don't overestimate myself.

I'm not sure people like Lucas ever truly acknowledge the harm they do, especially when they have an army of enablers around them, parents, lawyers, random girls online calling Erica a slut. Grown men too. Still, I get what she's saying.

"That's how we wish it could turn out, anyway," I acknowledge.

"I hope they won't blame Mr. McQuade. All her parents are trying to do is help her. They're not vigilantes."

"I don't think the police will go there." I try to assure her. "He had an alibi."

Merin is silent for a few seconds.

"I know I brushed you off when you first asked about Fiona and the other girls. I'm sorry. It wasn't that you didn't have a point. I...I found it disturbing."

"It is. I understand they're teenagers, and all of this is getting to them, but they're old enough to understand the gravity of the situation. Imagine going through a trauma like that, and your friends bail on you."

Merin shakes her head, frustrated. "That's not the Fiona I know, and I know Ellen didn't raise her that way. There must be something more. Maybe somebody threatened them."

"I think it's likely, but they aren't talking. Merin, the night after your birthday...the police stopped me."

"What for?" Her voice goes up a notch, alarm on her face.

"To tell me to stop asking questions. I'm not sure if it stops with Cross, or if it comes from higher up."

"This is serious! What are you going to do?"

"Nothing. I'm going home in a few days." It's not really a conversation I want to have at this time of night, but I can't avoid it. I have to admit I was distracted, having Merin all to myself for once, drinks, dance, and easy conversation... "There's something I need to show you." I get out of bed and rummage in my duffle bag until I find the small Ziploc bag with the earring.

"Is this yours?"

Merin's eyes widen. Oh my God. Does that mean what I'm afraid it means? Did Lucas do something to her sister, or her niece, and she shot him? But she wouldn't be able to move a dead body. Not on her own, anyway. Before I can spin this disturbing story any further, she says,

"I bought those for Fiona last Christmas. Where did you find it?"

"Something is wrong with all of this. It was in a bathroom, in the shack where Lucas was shot."

"Oh God," she whispers.

"My thoughts exactly. Does Fiona or her mother have access to a gun?"

This is all beyond worrisome, but I know how to interpret Merin's patient gaze.

"Yeah, of course they do," I say.

"You don't understand. We live pretty far out."

I don't think I'm ready for that conversation either.

"You told me about Gavin senior's inappropriate behavior. We know what Lucas did."

"No. Neither of them would do anything like that. They'd go to the police first. I heard what you said, but I would trust the sheriff to investigate a crime like this. They arrested Lucas, didn't they? Ellen and Fiona would know where to go if something happened to them. Killing somebody in revenge would not be their first instinct."

When I still don't respond, she continues, "I taught Sheriff Cross's children. He's not a bad man. LeBlanc and his buddies can be a nuisance, but I don't think Cross knows that they threatened you. And Liz Woodward. You've met Liz." Merin sounds a bit frantic at this point. "Not everyone here is a bigot or a killer."

Or both, I add silently.

"I didn't say that. We might not even know about everything Lucas did, or his father, for that matter. Someone from out of town might have had a beef with him."

"But you don't believe that."

"Honestly, I'm not sure what I believe, but we should talk to Ellen and Fiona."

Merin nods. At least we're back on the same page now. She still trusts me.

I didn't realize how much until she pushes back the covers, walks over to my bed and lies down next to me. Her initiating the contact, it makes all the difference in the world. I don't question it, just hold her close.

It's not cheating. Everyone needs to be close to someone when things get bad. If I'm right, they're only about to get worse.

⁓

Too soon, the warmth of her body against mine is only a memory. Merin is in the shower when I wake up. If she doesn't want to mention it, I won't. We didn't do anything wrong. In thought maybe, not in action.

She comes out of the bathroom, and I take my clothes with me as I go in.

In the breakfast room, we sit at a table by the window, looking out at endless fields.

Merin tastes her coffee with a sigh.

"I feel like I'm a horrible person. I know I'll have to have so many uncomfortable conversations now. I don't want this to end yet."

"That doesn't make you a horrible person," I assure her softly. I, too, want this moment of relative peace to last. For her. For both of us. "Only human."

"I wish I could believe that. But I'm still grateful for everything. If your offer still stands, I might take you up on it. The Bed & Breakfast by the ocean?"

"Oh yes, of course. I'll talk to Mom and Dad." I shouldn't be so excited about the prospect, knowing they could easily misunderstand the nature of our relationship, but I am.

"I think we need to head home."

"Okay, but let's finish breakfast. I'll call a cab to get us back to my car."

<hr />

In the room, we pack up our clothes, and I do a quick sweep of the wardrobe and drawers to make sure we didn't forget anything. When I straighten, Merin is standing right in front of me, too close, her expression both pleading and desperate.

I think I know how to read the message. If I go one step further, if it's me, then she won't feel so bad about herself. Because it wouldn't be her fault, would it? It would be so easy, and we'd end up back in that bed, giving up all reservations. I have more to show her than the only gay bar in town...but I can't. She's not ready, and I don't want her to end up hating me for pushing her over that line.

Friends. For now. She's still married, and neither one of us can forget about that.

"We got everything," I say, sounding a tad breathless. "Let's go."

For a brief moment, I wonder if it's worth risking everything to make the disappointment in her expression go away. I don't test the theory.

Chapter Seventeen

B ack in the bar's parking lot, looking at my car, I stand with my jaw dropping. Merin puts her hand over her mouth. Someone smashed in a window and a rear light and slashed the four tires. There was nothing in there worth stealing, which is a small silver lining. That's about the only thing to be optimistic about.

Was that person after something, or did they simply want to—again?—send a message? Did anyone object to the idea that I was here with Merin—which would mean they followed us?

A few hours ago, I almost thought George might have moved a dead body. But he's not that kind of two-faced person. If he didn't like me going out with his wife, he would have said it to my face, or hers.

"Okay. First of all, I'm so sorry," I say. It seems like a good way to start.

"That is definitely not your fault. Unless you had someone do this so you could spend more time with me?"

I appreciate her attempt at humor in this rather bleak situation.

"Believe me, I would have done that in more creative ways. And I'd love to spend more time with you. However..."

"I have the number of a garage in my phone," she says. "Let me call them for you."

I must have spaced out for a moment, because the next thing I know is that she hands the phone back to me, saying, "They'll be here in half an hour."

Do I contact the police? Who in that station can I trust?

"Ask for Officer Woodward or Sheriff Cross," Merin says as if reading my thoughts. I'm not sure if it will do any good, but I take her advice. To my relief, I reach Liz at the front desk, and she promises to send someone.

"You should call George. I can take care of the rest."

Merin hesitates before she answers. "He's at work right now. Team practice. I don't want to disturb him. Joe will bring us back to town, and they'll lend you a car for the time they need fixing yours."

"Are you sure?"

I'm not just talking about inconvenience. Joe from the garage, not to mention the police, will find us in the parking lot of a gay bar, a respected teacher and a suspicious newcomer in town. With overnight bags.

"You're making this out to be worse than it is. Whatever it is you're imagining right now, anyway. This," she points to the car, "*is* pretty bad."

"No kidding. All right then."

She's sensing that I'm not entirely convinced, and adds, "I'm serious. No one's going to give me any grief for helping out a friend."

I hope she's right, because we've added a whole lot of uncomfortable conversations to the list.

Small favors. Joe doesn't blink an eye at where we are. Liz Woodward pulls up in the squad car a few minutes after him. She and a colleague take pictures of the damage.

"You didn't see anything?" she asks.

"We weren't here," I say, a bit impatient with her approach. "But given where the car was parked, the motive is quite obvious, don't you think?"

"We'll do everything we can to find the person who did this, I promise you, Ms. Jameson." She keeps her tone neutral and professional.

"I'm sorry. I didn't mean to suggest otherwise." I believe Merin when she says that Officer Woodward doesn't know what some of her colleagues are up to. "You know where to find me."

"Yeah, I do. I'll let you know what we find." That sounds optimistic, but I'll take it.

Joe is towing the car and takes me and Merin back to town. We don't exchange a lot of words.

I sign up for a car to drive the next few days and finally drive Merin home. Part of me wishes I made different decisions earlier this morning. A part of me wants to get her out of here now. Threats, assault, murder, vandalism. How many crimes can happen in a town this small?

I guess I have a few days longer than planned to find out.

❦

Merin asks me inside and goes straight to the fridge where she inspects its contents.

"George won't be coming home until later this afternoon, so if we're going to do this, I was hoping you could help me make dinner."

"I'm happy to help you, but I think I need a little more information?"

"If we're going to talk to Ellen and Fiona? That's the plan, isn't it? Might as well soften the blow and serve them dinner first."

"Now I see where you're going. George won't mind after I already kidnapped you?"

She gives me a long look, and I shrug. "Still trying to get a feel for the dynamics. All right, dinner it is. I have to warn you, I'm not much of a cook. In fact, I don't cook."

"That's all right. You can chop a few things."

Merin opens the fridge again. "There's beer and wine too, good. I think that will help."

"Are you okay?" I ask.

She closes the door of the fridge and leans against the counter, as if giving my question some serious thought.

"If you are, I think I am. Let's just get through this, okay?"

I step forward and embrace her, my emotions still torn into every possible direction.

Come with me, let's go far away.

It's not enough to wish. She leans into me for a long, hopeful moment, then steps away. "We need to get started."

⁂

The wind has picked up, I notice, as I set the table in the dining room. All my time here, the bad weather the forecast predicted has stayed somewhat at bay, some rain, thunder, and then it's back to the hot and humid weather. Signs of something bigger to come—and I'm still here.

Merin has prepared a roast chicken dinner after inviting Fiona and her parents. She exchanged a couple of text messages with George who is on his way. I wonder if our little adventure has already made the rounds in town, if this will backfire on Merin, and how I could make things right.

George arrives at the same time as the guests. Everyone is polite, except Fiona's expression tells me she doesn't like me here.

"Thanks for coming over," Merin says after everyone has been provided with drinks, iced tea for Fiona. "I guess by now you heard we were caught in the parking lot of a gay bar. We had left the car there. Someone vandalized Kelli's car."

If they had additional questions as to the scene of the crime, no one's asking them at the moment.

"Merin! Why didn't you tell me earlier?"

"I'm telling you now," she says to her husband. "We weren't there when they did it, so there was never any danger. It's annoying nonetheless, but this is not why we asked you all to come here."

They look from her to me, and back, waiting in tense silence.

"All right, here it goes," I begin. "Fiona, I think we all need to know why your earring was found in the place where Lucas was shot."

"What? That's not possible!" Her cheeks redden. "What is this, anyway?"

"What is she talking about?" Ellen asks, alarm showing on her face.

We are met with stubborn silence.

"Fiona, your aunt is worried about you," I remind her.

"There's no reason. I lost the earring a while ago. I didn't want to tell you, Merin, because I thought you'd be disappointed. Maybe someone picked it up."

"To drop it at a murder scene? Why would they do that?"

"For the same reason they're making some people think you might be the one who shot him?" she fires back at me.

"Fiona!" Ellen chastises.

"It's true," Fiona defends herself. "One of the guys in class is LeBlanc's brother. He says that they took your gun."

"They didn't keep it. They just wanted to look at the paper-work, and I got it back. You have a gun in the house?"

"What are you saying?" Merin's sister isn't happy with the implications. "Merin, I'm not sure we should have this conversation right now."

"I trust Kelli. She stays," Merin insists. "She saved Fiona from Bradley."

Fiona huffs at that. "I can take care of myself."

This is not the time to argue.

"Okay. So, you don't know how your earring ended up in the shack?"

"I swear. I'm sorry I was careless with it, but I don't go in the woods all the time."

"Does Lexi? I saw her there the other day."

Fiona looks resigned all of a sudden, and I'm certain she's on the verge of revealing something.

"Look. It has nothing to do with Lucas. I swear we weren't there that night. In fact, we haven't been back since early this year."

"What were you doing there? This thing is about to fall down." Her mother sounds alarmed.

I think she has reason to be, whatever the answer is.

"Don't be mad, okay? Like I said, we haven't been back in a long time, and I don't think any of us will ever want to go there again. We went to this place sometimes to…have some wine, or smoke pot."

"What?" Ellen's voice rises. Merin and George share a worried look. "Why would you do that?"

"What do you think? To try it…and it's been pretty stressful around here."

I don't have all the pieces yet, but a picture is starting to emerge.

"Did Erica go with you sometimes? To drink and smoke pot?"

I know I'm on to something when Fiona avoids my gaze. Catching herself, she looks back at me. "Once or twice. She was always afraid we would get caught, paranoid, so the last few times, we didn't tell her."

The last few times. How many times?

"Maybe you should have listened to her," Merin mumbles.

"Did Lucas, Pete, or anyone of their friends know about this?"

Fiona shrugs. "I don't know. Maybe."

"Do we have to tell the police?" George wonders out loud. "If they found DNA..."

Having seen some of their work, I'm not sure how serious the effort was. The Gavins might have put pressure, but not to find the real shooter. They just want someone to blame, and I'm not sure how willing Cross is to go along with it.

I can still feel the concrete scraping my palms and knees. I've had worse, but for a brief moment I was afraid how far they might go. No, I'm not ready to deliver them Fiona.

"I think we can avoid that for now," I say. "You, Lexi, and Amanda need to stay away from that place. And it's not a good idea to walk in the woods at night."

"Yeah, right, because you could be raped." Fiona's gaze is defiant now. "It's on us to be careful. Then again, that could happen at a party, so why bother?"

I feel her anger and frustration, so much.

"I agree with you. You should be safe walking in the woods at any time, at a party...at work." There's no mistaking the grim expression on Ellen's face. "But there was a shooter in the woods, and we don't know what their motivation was. If they wanted to punish Lucas, the rest of the town might be safe. If it was random, everyone could be in danger."

"You think it could be a woman?" George asks. "I heard those boys had trouble with drugs...harder stuff than pot," he hurries to say, and Fiona rolls her eyes in typical teenage fashion.

"Whoever did it, they were pretty angry at Lucas Gavin," I say. There's this curious overlap, people talking about drugs the "boys" did. Fiona and her friends meeting to smoke pot.

It's a small town. I don't think they have multiple dealers at their disposal.

"Many people would have a reason." I want to ask her about who was their dealer, though this might be a bit too much before dinner.

"Well, no one at this table did it," Fiona says. "Is there going to be food at some point?"

Ellen shakes her head, but she doesn't comment.

"Don't worry, there's plenty," Merin says with a smile that's a tad too cheery for the setting. "George?"

Of course she'd ask her husband to help, not me.

Why would that even be a surprise?

Chapter Eighteen

Merin

I feel feverish, which could be for so many reasons. The constant heat, my insane idea of making a chicken dinner for discussing matters that have all of us on the edge. It's been like that for some time now, even before Kelli came to town.

Kelli.

I can barely look at her, and that might be the reason why I haven't stopped since we returned from our night away.

When did we all go so wrong?

The day Lucas decided he wouldn't take no for an answer? Or long before that, when his parents taught him that when you have enough money to make it all go away, you can do whatever you want? My head is spinning.

Too much wine.

Too much of everything.

"Be careful," George warns when I open the door of the oven. I take a deep breath, and it's all I can do not to snap at him. I've been careful my whole life, especially from the moment I've experienced attractions that wouldn't go over well with my family or my employer.

Is he careful? All the time? Because whenever one of us steps out of the comfortable pretense, we play with our reputations, our livelihoods, for what?

I didn't get it before, but I think I do now. Not because Kelli keeps telling me about what I deserve, or because she showed me the niche George has already carved out for himself.

Last night broke something within me, the self-righteous resistance that has kept me safe so far.

I'm irrationally mad at her because she respects my boundaries. I'm the one who crawled into her bed last night, and all she did was hold me. I spent that time feeling safe and happy, and I hated having to give it up again.

What if she's right? What if I can't trust the people that I've known all my life? I know the way most people in town talked when gay marriage became legal. Equal marriage, Kelli would certainly call it. *What's next?* I heard someone say. *People marrying their toaster?*

As if we were an object for daily use.

It's of no use to think about marriage, gay or straight, anyone's. Kelli is going home, and she should, because it's not safe for her. I still can't imagine Sheriff Cross signing off on intimidation tactics, but it only takes a bad apple or two, the vandalized car a case in point.

I need to get dinner on the table.

Is it safe for anyone?

Is there a criminal with a gun running around in town?

A drug dealer seeking revenge?

I wish I was the kind of person who can just pack up and start over somewhere else. George gives me a hesitant smile, and I wonder if he'd agree to a divorce, not that it's realistic at all.

"Let's get this on the table," I say.

When I come back to the kitchen to make coffee, Kelli follows me.

"How do you think it went?" she asks.

It's harder like this, being alone with her in a confined space. And she thought taking me to a gay bar would make a difference? The truth has been wearing away at me steadily over the past weeks.

It works for some couples if you're on the same page. It's nobody's business but your own. Except Joe knows, and Liz Woodward, and God knows how many people who recognized George on one of his dates. I'm not really mad at him, or Kelli. I'm just so tired.

"As well as expected," I say with a shrug. "I think Ellen will be glad not to deal with the police, but Fiona will be grounded for some time to come."

"Yeah. Imagine a teenager sneaking out in the woods to drink and smoke pot."

"She's her mother. There need to be some consequences. Besides, I never did that."

Kelli's smile tells me she believes me.

"What? You had a false ID?"

"Not me, but one of my friends. Not that it matters now..." She trails off when Fiona enters the kitchen and leans against the counter.

"I guess now you know my big bad secret."

"Thank you for trusting us."

Fiona's expression says it all. I don't blame her—she didn't have much of a choice. But everything we're doing here is for the greater good, isn't it? Even with all the painful memories and truths we have to evoke.

"I get it now," Kelli continues, her voice soft. "You thought you were doing Erica a favor. If they had found out about your secret, they would have used it to discredit her, and you."

"I guess. They did so anyway, so there wasn't much of a point to it. After it became clear that Lucas was killed there, we couldn't go back."

"Who was your dealer?" The same soft, seductive tone, I almost miss the sharp edge of the question. Fiona does too, her wince a delayed reaction. It occurs to me that Kelli isn't new to this, interrogating suspects, though I assume it's part of the PI job.

Fiona doesn't try to correct the term. "A boy in school. I don't know where he gets it from."

"What's his name?"

"You promise you won't do anything? Go to the police? This, Mom can't know."

"I'm not going to tell anyone," Kelli says quickly. Perhaps she understands I can't make the same promise. Fiona seems so relieved to finally be able to talk to someone that she's not paying much attention to detail.

"It's Adam Bradley. Pete's brother."

"For Christ's sake!" I slap my hand against my mouth, though this justifies swearing. No wonder Kelli thinks the whole town is corrupt. There is no way Pete and Kyle don't know about what's been going on at the shack. Likely, Lucas did too. What were they thinking?

"Is that why you met with Pete the other night?" Kelli asks. She hangs her head.

"Adam claims we still owe him money. It's not true."

"So, he sends his big brother to intimidate you. How courageous," Kelli comments.

"Fiona, this isn't working," I say. "You can't deal with these things on your own."

"I'm talking to you now, aren't I? Besides, look what happened to Erica. She can barely leave the house. No, I think we've dealt with things pretty well so far."

"Your aunt is right," Kelli says, and for some reason, I'm not happy she's calling me that. This is not the time.

"Are you going to do something about all this? Look, I'm grateful you bailed me out with Pete, but you can't be around all the time."

That's what I'm afraid of. I can tell from Kelli's expression that she knows Fiona has a point, and she hates it just as much as I do.

"At some point, someone needs to get to these corrupt families," she says, sounding frustrated.

"Good luck with that. Can we have dessert now, please?"

I'm not sure how much we have really solved tonight, but it's a beginning, right? Fiona and Ellen leave first. There's an awkward moment when I wish it could be George leaving instead of Kelli, awkward because I fear both of them can sense it.

Then the door closes behind her, and I turn to the kitchen with a heavy heart.

"Merin, wait."

"We have a load of dishes to rinse," I say. When he doesn't answer, I turn to him. "I'd prefer we do it now rather than tomorrow."

"Is there something we should talk about first?"

"No." I don't want to, and what good would it do? It's not going to change anything. *We* aren't going to change anything.

"Are you sure? You spent the night with her." There's no scolding, just genuine curiosity.

"It wasn't...Not what you think. And yes, I know how that sounds." Lying in her arms, wishing I could wake up like this every morning, that wasn't cheating. That was just me coming to the end of my ability to hold it all together.

"I'm not judging."

No, you couldn't.

"We've always been honest, right? And we want to keep it that way."

He asked for it, didn't he?

"Sure." I'm doing my best not to snap. "What do you want to know? I haven't had sex with her, and it's not because I didn't want to. It's because I remembered my wedding vows."

He looks like I've slapped him, and maybe that was my intention. I *am* a horrible person.

George reaches out to touch my cheek, and I shrink away.

"Not now. You don't have to worry, nothing has changed. You can do what you want. I'm going to get those dishes into the dishwasher."

He doesn't object.

I wish there was someone I could talk to, but no one in my family would understand. I've brushed off someone who used to be my best friend.

That leaves Kelli...

It's too dangerous. I might never come back, and that thought is still scarier than anything.

The next day, we have dinner with George's parents. He has gauged my mood correctly and not raised any difficult questions. George's sister is visiting from out of town with her husband Jeb and their two kids.

I remember how they used to do the friendly nagging, about when we would have children. No one has asked in a long time, though I know they're still talking about it, wondering what's wrong. It was one of George and Carol's cousins who made that stupid pun about marrying a toaster. Everyone laughed.

"Merin, are you okay? You look a little pale," Carol observes.

"I'm fine. It's just the heat getting to me."

"Are you sure that's all?"

"What do you want me to say?" I snap, all eyes on me in an instant.

"Sorry," she says, offended. "It's hot for all of us."

"I'm sorry. I didn't mean…"

"Forget about it. Let's just enjoy dinner." One of her girls is putting both hands in the mashed potatoes, and she's instantly distracted from my less than polite ways. Her husband doesn't raise a finger.

In terms of marriage, I still win.

For the rest of the meal, I cling to my wine and tune out the conversation. I'm jolted back in when my mother-in-law mentions Kelli.

"I don't want to believe every rumor, but isn't it strange that she's still here? Mr. and Mrs. Gavin wanted her to find Lucas. Now that we know…George, hasn't she been to your house a few times?"

"She has," he says. "Maybe she likes it here."

"Oh, I doubt that after her car got totaled."

My parents and George's parents go to the same church. They hear the same gossip. Someone will ask me about the parking lot sometime soon.

"It wasn't totaled," I clarify. "Someone smashed a window and one of the lights and slashed the tires." I might as well get ahead of them. I catch George's gaze, the hint of impatience in his expression. *Now you want to do this?* I can almost hear the question.

I don't. I don't want to stir up conflict and confrontation, find out if the people closest to me would still talk to me if they knew. It scares the hell out of me, and that might not even be an exaggeration. Maybe I will go to Hell, but not for wanting more than the life I have now. Maybe lies and pretense are the bigger sin?

"It could be related to her work...or someone homophobic."

"Homophobic?" Carol echoes. She says the word as if trying out a term in a foreign language for the first time. Foreign, I'm sure it is to her.

George shakes his head at me.

He's right. This is not me. Raising my voice, causing trouble. Besides, I'm not the only one who has a lot on the line.

"I don't know for sure," I say. "I'm sure the police are going to find out who did it."

"Yes, let's let them do their job," Jeb agrees, and somehow steers the conversation to football statistics. George, now looking relieved, and his father join in.

What did I do?

❦

I might have outed Kelli tonight, without her consent, and I came close to doing the same to George and myself. What is wrong with me? Once this is all over, all I'll be left with are a phone number, a beautiful bracelet, and my pitiful lack of courage. I can't mess up my life and take the people I love down with me—because it's still true, I do love him. He's been more than a cover story to me.

I thought we were doing the right thing, because the people who matter to us couldn't handle the truth. Our community. But it's the same community where a lot of people felt sorry for a rapist and blamed the victim.

They tried to frame a stranger for murder because it's convenient, because the Gavins pulled strings.

What do we owe them, really?

I don't know anymore.

I start crying in the car—*pitiful*. Once home, George closes the door behind us and pulls me close. A friendly embrace. It's not what I want, but apparently, it's all I can get tonight.

"I know you're going through a tough time right now, but we need to be careful."

"I know that."

I don't want to be careful. For once I want to be selfish, do something that serves me and only me.

"Will you keep seeing that guy?"

"Liam. His name is Liam, and I've been seeing him for the past four years." His tone is gentle, and somehow that makes everything worse.

When he first told me, I didn't ask many questions. That way, I could simply ignore his existence. Part of me wants it to stay that way, but it's impossible. It's not just between the two of us—and Liam—any longer.

What does he think of the arrangement?

The heart of the matter—what do I even want?

"Merin, I need to know if we're still on the same page. We've said we're doing this because it's worth it, so that we can keep our careers and lives. I'm not sure what exactly happened, but Kelli is going back home soon, right? You're telling me you want to go with her?"

I want that so much. I can't.

"I don't think she wants to deal with this mess." That's not a real answer, and he knows it.

"We have a good life, don't we?" He's pleading for me to understand. "Let's not put that at risk."

I can't talk to him right now. I'm still too confused, and angry, even though I know it's not all his fault. I'm afraid I might say things I'd regret.

"I have to go."

"You're going to see her?"

"Are you going to tell me I can't?" I challenge him.

George throws his hands up in the air. "Do what you want. I'll see you later."

I pick up my purse and leave. Once in my car, I drive straight to the hotel. I have no idea what I'm going to say, or how this is going to play out, but I don't hesitate, walk the stairs up to Kelli's room and knock. And again.

"Kelli? Are you there?"

No answer.

Of all the things I imagined, this wasn't one of them. What now?

There are footsteps behind me, and I spin around, almost colliding with Officer Liz Woodward. When I see the serious expression on her face, my heart skips a beat.

"What are you doing here? Did something happen to Kelli?"

"Ms. Jameson? No," she says, and I sink back against the door, sighing in relief. "Mrs. Burke, do you know where she is? I need to talk to her. I'm afraid I have to tell you...Fiona is missing."

Just like that, every nightmare becomes possible again, making my own woes irrelevant instantly.

Chapter Nineteen

I realize I left my phone at home when I all but stormed out. Liz lets me use hers to send an urgent text. I'm trying not to drown in a maelstrom of worst-case scenarios. Kelli will be fine. Fiona will be fine. I can make myself believe that as long as I ignore that a girl was raped not long ago, and the rapist who got off with barely a slap on the wrist, turned up dead. Broken glass in the parking lot, threats from a police officer.

"Do you want a ride with me?" Liz asks. "You could get your car later."

"No, thank you, I'll be okay." Will I be? This is not about me. "I need to talk to Ellen."

"Of course. I'll let you know as soon as I know more," she promises when we walk back to our respective cars.

"Liz, wait a second."

"I need to get going," she says, as if sensing that I'm about to raise an uncomfortable subject. At the moment, I couldn't care less about her comfort. I won't take chances with the lives of the people I care about.

"You know that LeBlanc and his buddy threatened Kelli?"

"That was stupid, but they're not serious. They're friends with Bradley."

"Excuse me if that doesn't make me feel better. What about Sheriff Cross? Can I trust him to give a damn about my niece, and Kelli?"

"I'll do whatever I can."

"That's not an answer and you know it."

"Cross and LeBlanc are still working on the homicide with the detective from the county. I swear there are still people who are doing their jobs. I think you know what it's like to be under the radar."

"What's that supposed to mean?"

"You know what it means," she says with a shrug. "I have to go."

I drive back home only to find the house empty. George has left me a note on the kitchen counter, right next to my phone.

I'm over at Ellen's. Call me.

I skip the request and go right back out, this time with my phone in my purse. When I arrive at Ellen's, there's a police car parked outside their property, the sight sending a chill down my spine. That makes it real. I haven't had time to talk to Kelli since we made Fiona confess about the girls' secret activities. Didn't we take her seriously enough? Did she tell us the whole truth?

I all but run to the front door and knock. It's George who opens the door, looking dejected.

"No news?" I ask anyway.

"Not on Fiona," he says, and I walk past him into the living room where Ellen is sitting on the couch, crying. Her husband Drew is next to her, making a futile attempt at comforting her.

Sheriff Cross is standing in a corner, talking to...Kelli? She comes right over when she sees me, but I shake my head and turn to my sister.

"What happened? I saw Liz, she told me Fiona is missing."

Ellen looks up at me. I'm struck by the despair in her eyes. Does she know more than I do?

"It's all your fault!" she accuses. I nearly take a step back.

"Now, let's not do this." Kelli is next to me within a heartbeat.

I put a hand on her arm to convey that I can handle this—and only for that reason, but all of a sudden, I feel like everyone in the room is staring.

"I told her she was grounded, and she ran away! This would have never happened if you'd just left it alone."

We all need to be careful about what we say next, with the sheriff in the room.

"How about we sort out all of this once we have found Fiona?"

"I got a team out there," Cross says. "We'll find her, Ellen."

"Did you talk to Amanda and Lexi?" I ask.

"Officer Woodward did. They don't know where she is."

I should stay here, support my sister and her family, but I wonder if I could be more useful somewhere else. It always seems to come down to Bradley, Lucas's key witness, who pulls strings. Who already threatened her, and not much came of it. I'm so tired of everyone acting like some people are and should be above the law.

"I can talk to them again," I offer. "Those girls are best friends. Even if she didn't tell them, they might have an idea."

"I'll come with you," Kelli says, and to my surprise, no one protests. It's as if they have already written me off—but I'll chalk it up to the anguish they feel. What else would it be?

"Where have you been?" I ask when we are in the car, and she's pulling out of the parking spot. If it sounds needy, I don't care.

"Wrapping up things. Trying, anyway." Kelli's answer is a lot more vague than I hoped for. "How are you?"

"Honestly? I don't even know anymore," I admit. "I try not to panic. It's difficult."

"I understand. I also understand that Ellen is scared, but she shouldn't talk to you like that. They're underage. It's not like we could just ignore what they did."

I'm not sure if she meant it, or if it was a slip of the tongue, but I'm warmed by the mere concept of "we" in this mess.

"So where do we go first?"

"Pete Bradley," she says. "I'm worried that the sheriff won't do much about him."

"After LeBlanc warned you to leave him alone?"

"After this is all over, a lot of people will rethink what they said."

How can she be so sure?

"I'm scared," I say, my voice embarrassingly close to breaking—again. "Of what might have happened to her."

"I know." Kelli reaches out to touch my hand. She doesn't make any false promises. That's a comfort in itself.

Kelli parks the car in front of the Bradleys' estate, where Pete has been hiding out after getting released on bail.

"You don't have to come in," she says. I know she means well, though it only serves to remind me that I'll be the one staying behind.

Left behind. No, that's not fair. She gave me choices. The problem is the choice was made for me a long time ago, wasn't it? In any case, whatever damage she's worried about, is probably already done. This is about Fiona. I'll worry about my reputation later.

Pete's parents are not home, the housekeeper tells us.

"Is Pete here?" I ask. "We need to talk to him."

She looks hesitant, but eventually nods. "I'll see if he's available." Kelli looks down, and I'm pretty sure she's rolling her eyes, not at the woman, but Pete Bradley who thinks he's so damn important.

The housekeeper returns after what feels like an eternity. Probably not more than ten minutes have passed by. Nonetheless, the message is clear: He keeps us waiting because he can.

I taught Pete for a while, same with all the young people involved in this tragic story, but I've never been to his home. George and I aren't the kind of folks the Bradleys socialize with.

"Please follow me," the housekeeper says quietly. She takes us down an impressive staircase and along a hallway, then knocks on a door at the end of it.

"Mr. Bradley? Mrs. Burke is here."

I catch Kelli's gaze on me. I don't know if she's surprised or impressed. I'm not sure what's going to happen in a minute.

It's no surprise that Pete keeps us waiting again.

"Mrs. Burke, to what do I owe the pleasure?" he asks as he opens the door. "Is something wrong?"

I want to punch him. He knows I'm Fiona's aunt. He knows I'm angry.

"Cut the crap, Bradley. Have you seen Fiona?" Kelli asks.

"You two are too funny," he says, laughing. "I thought I wasn't supposed to go near her."

"You're not," I say. "She's missing. You threatened her only a few days ago."

"Whatever. I got arrested, and as you can see, I got out. With conditions. I don't care about the b—well, I don't know where she is," he catches himself.

This might be a waste of time. Kelli doesn't seem to think so, because she walks past him into the room, and for the lack of an alternative, I follow her. I stop cold when I realize Pete has friends with him, including Kyle Vance. They are playing a round of pool. Kyle comes over to us.

"Mrs. Burke, what a surprise."

"Is it?" Kelli asks sharply.

"What's that supposed to mean?" Bradley's polite mask slips quickly. "Frankly, I'm tired of this shit. None of us knows where your niece is, to be honest, none of us cares. Now leave us alone, or I'll call the police."

"Your friend LeBlanc? He can't always protect you."

"Interesting."

For a moment, he steps so close our noses are almost touching. "Just like this one can't always protect you, huh?"

"Leave her alone," Kelli snaps and takes my arm. "Come on."

The housekeeper who has been silently waiting outside, walks us out, her composure showing her discomfort.

"This is unbelievable," Kelli says when we are out of her earshot. "I'll stay as long as you need me here."

"Isn't your boss going to want you back at some point?" Even in the midst of this chaotic situation, I can't ignore the flutter of hope. Misplaced, maybe, but real.

"I'll figure something out. Seriously, what were they doing? There were beer bottles. Celebrating something?"

"Bradley's release? I don't know. Should we see Amanda and Lexi next?"

I check my phone. No message from Ellen or Liz Woodward.

"Yes, let's do that." She sighs. "I understand they weren't that interested in helping to find Lucas Gavin, but this is different, right? They're Fiona's friends."

I used to think so. Before Erica. Now I don't know what to think. All I want is for Fiona to be home, safe and sound.

Chapter Twenty

Kelli

I'm serious. Tempers are running high right now, and I'm not going to leave her alone. I can't keep complaining about this town and not do anything that's in my power to help the decent people here, right? It's not exactly in the job description, but it's the most important thing.

"When I left your place the other day, I saw Fiona leaving the house shortly after she and Ellen had arrived. She met with Lexi and Amanda at Lexi's."

Merin's eyes widen. "Did you tell the sheriff?"

"Not yet. I want to see what they have to say."

"Isn't that a big risk? The police have resources that we don't have."

"The cops might also be in the Gavins' and the Bradleys' pockets. Adam Bradley will probably get away with a slap on the wrist, if it even comes to that, but the girls could be in trouble over the pot and the drinking."

She leans back in her seat with a sigh.

"This is a nightmare."

"It is." It's been from the beginning, with few hopeful moments. I wonder what conversations she and George have had at this point, but now is not the time.

We pull up at Amanda's house. Her eyes are red-rimmed when she opens the door to us. A gust of wind almost slams it into our faces.

"Have you found Fiona yet?" she asks.

"Not yet. Can we talk to you for a second?"

With a resigned shrug, she lets us in. "Whatever."

It doesn't surprise me that we find Lexi in her room. Unlike Bradley and Vance, they are not in a celebratory mood.

"I know what you're going to ask," Lexi greets us. "We wish we knew. We have asked everyone, but she just...vanished."

No one can just vanish in this town, unless...Fiona isn't in town anymore. I can't believe that one argument with her mother led her to jump into a stranger's car and leave. There's always been something a lot more deliberate about the girls' actions. They might not know where she is, but I'm sure they have insights into her thinking that we don't.

"You talked to her the other day, about your meetings at the shack."

Lexi stares back at me defiantly. "Yes, she told us all about how you made her tell, in front of everybody."

"It's not safe out there," Merin says. "We're worried about Fiona, and all of you."

Lexi shrugs. "We can take care of ourselves."

"Like Fiona? Like Lucas?" I challenge.

"That's not the same! He raped someone, so who cares if he's dead?" There, she said it out loud. As adults, we can't be this bold. There's the law, and there's our own discomfort with vigilante justice, much as we might accept and even appreciate it in fiction. This isn't fiction. A man is dead, and the other theory is related to drugs. His friend's younger brother is dealing. Their respective parents all but own this town.

"Okay, that's not the question right now. We want to find Fiona." I hesitate to go much further than that in front of Merin. It's all theory at this point, but it comes down to two different paths, and in neither one of them did Fiona leave freely. Whether this is about drugs or Lucas's crime—crimes?—she might be in danger either way, from someone who doesn't want her to talk.

I think of the people who were in the room: Ellen and her husband, George, Sheriff Cross. The latter being the only one who's not family, and lukewarm about going after the real criminals.

"Look, I know things have been tough around here for some time. I might be able to bring in help from out of town, but you need to be honest with me."

"How would you be able to help us with anything? We're just all keeping our heads down until we can leave for college," Lexi says.

I catch Merin's thoughtful gaze. Is she wondering if there's a way out for her as well? Also: What a terrible way to live.

"What were you talking about the other day?"

"What we're always talking about. School. Pop stars."

"Are you kidding me? One of your friends is raped, you turn a cold shoulder. Now another one is missing, and you act like it's no big deal either? What is wrong with you?"

"Kelli." Merin's shocked tone does little to divert me.

Amanda's eyes are welling up while Lexi snaps at me, "You have no idea what you're talking about!"

"Then tell me. Fiona's life might depend on it."

She cast an uncertain look at Merin.

"Don't look at me. I'm here as Fiona's aunt, not your teacher. If there's something you have to say, say it now."

143

The two girls share another look. It's unnerving. Finally, Lexi speaks,

"Pete was pissed at us because his brother said we owe him money. This was all blown way out of proportion. We smoked a joint a couple of times, and one time, someone's older sibling bought a six pack and a bottle of wine. But Adam kept coming back. He wanted to sell. Other stuff too."

"So, they knew where you were meeting?"

"I don't know. We didn't tell them, but it probably wasn't that hard to find out. We were just trying to get away from it all, what happened with Erica."

"Fiona said you thought keeping your distance would help Erica?"

That one is still hard to understand.

"If you really can help, do it," Lexi says. "Pete is up to something. He's done everything Adam and Lucas did, and he got away with it too. There was never even a trial."

I hope I haven't promised too much, but this can't go on much longer. I've done everything I could. It's time to call in the cavalry.

⚬⚬⚬

When we come back outside, I'm surprised how the sky has darkened. I'll have to make some calls, but I want to check something first. As much as I like being with Merin, she shouldn't be around for either of it.

"I should drop you off at home," I say. There's thunder in the distance. Not much time to argue. I hope Fiona is somewhere safe, but I'm afraid that's wishful thinking.

"I don't want to go."

"There's something I need to do. The weather is getting worse."

She shakes her head with a wry laugh. "I grew up around here. Try again."

"Drugs, rape, murder. Is it so bad that I don't want you near any of it?"

A smile softens her features. She doesn't back down though.

"I don't want you, or my niece near any of it, but here we are. I can't go home now. What's the plan?"

"That depends on whether we believe in asking for permission or forgiveness. I need to call my boss. We're going to sneak into Bradley's house."

"We need to find Fiona," she says, her tone revealing every emotion.

"We will," I promise. "Let's go."

I'm not sure if we'll be able to find forgiveness from anyone after this, but a life at stake supersedes every doubt.

<hr>

The bad weather that's been promised to us for some time now is on its way. The sky is further darkening with ominous gray clouds, and it's starting to rain, not that it has much impact on the temperature.

"They forecast a big storm for later today," Merin says.

"I can still drive by your house and drop you off."

"No, we'll lose too much time. If we don't find anything, we'll go straight home from here, and you'll stay with us until it's passed. George won't mind."

"Are you sure?"

She checks her phone. "He's still with Ellen. So, what's the plan? How do we get in?"

"Check for a window or a door that isn't locked? They were drinking. I'm pretty sure at this point they're loaded. They won't even realize."

Merin casts me a look I can't quite interpret. It's somewhere in between apprehensive and admiring.

"I would like to tell you to stay in the car, but I think it's better if we don't split up. I'll park the car in the distance."

"When you told the girls earlier that you could bring in help, did you really mean it?"

"I did," I say, aware that we are entering dangerous territory, and not just because we crossed the line to the Bradleys' property. With a little luck, this will be quick. They must not expect Mr. and Mrs. Bradley back today, or they wouldn't throw their little party, alcohol included. I'm sure the parents won't even notice. They either bribed or pressured the housekeeper to look the other way.

"What do you hope we're going to find?"

My luck, Merin is not pressing me on the details of the "help." But the answer she's asking for is not an easy one either. Those guys were stupidly loyal to Lucas. If they are holding Fiona…I don't want to think of the worst-case scenario, but it's hard not to.

"Any proof of wrongdoing. Lies. Something to hold over them."

She doesn't disagree with my assessment, but we both know that might take a while.

"Make that call first?"

"I think that's a good idea."

❦

It's beyond strange to speak to my boss with Merin by my side, the two lives I've been living colliding like I always knew they would one day.

146

"There is evidence of some long-term serious misconduct by the sheriff's office, but I'll fill you in on that later. A girl is missing, and we can't trust locals on this. I need some help."

To my relief, he doesn't try to argue. I detail what I need.

"I can make some calls. Someone from the county could join you tomorrow," he says.

"That's...late. I need some confirmation today. We're at Bradley's house."

"You're sure that they have her?"

"It would make sense," I say, aware of Merin studying me curiously.

"You'll have to wait for the warrant."

"Sure."

"Damn it, Jameson, you remember why you're there in the first place?"

"I haven't forgotten. This girl might be in danger, and the sheriff and a few of his officers are more interested in covering for the family."

"Wait for the warrant." He punctuates every word clearly. "You have your phone with you?"

"You're doing this now?" I ask, dumbfounded.

"It's an emergency, that's what you're telling me, right?"

"Yes, sir. Thank you."

"That sounds like you have a lot of people at your disposal," Merin says. "I always imagined PIs working in an office with a few colleagues."

"I'll tell you later. For now, let's just take a look around outside."

It occurs to me that this will be the point of no return—and afterwards, Merin might reconsider whether she wants to visit me at my parents'.

Chapter Twenty-One

T he wind has picked up, tearing at our clothes, and the rain has gotten stronger as well. The storm was announced for tonight, but now we can already hear the thunder close by. One way or another, the air will be cleared.

As we near the Bradleys' property once more, I realize that there are fewer cars now. The truck belongs to Pete. Are his friends gone? What does that mean?

"I don't want you to think I'm scared. I'm not," Merin says. "But we're not here for papers, right? We're not going to take anything?"

She has to raise her voice over the storm as we're hiding behind some high and probably expensive bushes. I realize that even if I wanted to, I couldn't send her away right now.

"It will be okay!" We can only hope to make it back to her place in time. No message from the boss. We come to the back of the house.

The sound of the wind has become alarming, but I still hear the other noise over it, a consistent bang of metal against metal.

"What is that?" Merin asks.

"I don't know, but we're going to find out."

It takes me a few seconds to realize the sound is coming from a structure I have only seen on the Internet before. Shouldn't there be a way you could get out from the inside, even if someone locked the door from outside? It's only now that I see the huge padlock. Merin has turned pale.

"We need to open this."

"How did you know...?"

"A guess," I say. "After what the girls told us...She seems okay in there, making noise. Let's get her out." The warrant can wait. We have to get to Fiona, make sure she isn't hurt.

"Let's get Bradley. This, he can't get himself out of so easily."

"Don't get your hopes up too high."

I spin around to see Pete Bradley standing there with a rifle. The same that killed Lucas, I wonder? Did Pete rape Erica? Did Lucas want to go to the authorities?

"Don't do anything stupid," I warn. "We can talk about this. You need to let her out."

"What, you're going to make me? There's a reason why she's in there. She's the dangerous one, and until Sheriff Cross can come here, she'll stay. Crazy bitches didn't tell you they murdered my best friend, huh?"

"Pete, come on, that's ridiculous," Merin snaps.

He's distracted for the moment long enough for me to get to my gun and point it at him.

"I'm Detective Jameson, Peter Bradley, you're under arrest for kidnapping. Drop the gun. Now!" I yell over the wind as I realize he's dumbfounded.

Merin's expression is impassive. Now's not the moment to be distracted.

"Drop the gun, Bradley!" He finally does, but then something crashes down from the porch. He takes advantage and runs. It has to end. I'm angry and frustrated with how little I've been able to achieve, maybe even frustrated for other reasons, but I can't let him get away now.

Whatever he and Lucas did, what the sheriff and his men covered up, it will all come to light now. And maybe, after all this time, even the McQuades can get some peace.

I tackle him right into one of the bushes that Merin and I hid behind earlier, wrenching his arms behind his back.

"You're all in on it!" he huffs. "You're going to prison once the sheriff finds out."

"I wouldn't count on it," I say as I'm cuffing him, one of the most satisfying actions since I've set foot in this town. "Backup is on the way. You'll have a lot to answer for."

"Backup?" He laughs. "Where is that coming from? The storm is moving here faster than expected, and they said there might be tornadoes. No one in their right mind is getting out on the road now."

I hate to admit it, but he has a point. Where do we go from here?

"Let me worry about. Now where's the key to that padlock?"

I get nothing but stubborn silence from him until Merin speaks.

"Yes, tell her, Pete. I'd really like to see my niece again." I get to my feet, coming face to face with her holding the rifle.

"Whoa, careful with that."

"Don't worry, I can handle it. Now get up!"

Pete struggles to his feet, alarm in his expression. "You're going to kill me too?"

Merin shakes her head. "Don't be ridiculous. No one's going to kill anyone. The keys—now!"

"In my back pocket! You're a real cop?" he addresses me as I retrieve them and open the lock. "Then you need to ask Fiona some questions. She doesn't have an alibi for the night Lucas disappeared."

"That doesn't mean anything," Merin says.

I think of the girls calling him a coward. His fear seems real, then again, he's the one who covered for his rapist buddy and his drug-dealing brother. All those other stories are nothing but wild accusations.

The decision about what to do next is taken out of our hands when the sirens sound. I realize that the sky has turned almost black. Lightning cracks.

Fiona leaves her temporary prison pale but looking otherwise unharmed. She hugs Merin tightly.

"Thank you so much for looking for me. You, too, Kelli. I just want to go home."

"Yes, let's go home," I say, relieved, even though it means we have to bring Pete in the backseat.

Merin shakes her head. "Trust me when I say no one is going anywhere. If you try to outrun a tornado, you could get yourself killed. Let's all wait here until it's over."

Pete is the first to stumble down the stairs, and I have no choice but to follow.

I'll have to trust the people who have spent all their lives here.

Chapter Twenty-Two

Merin

I sent a quick text message to Ellen, which I hope will go through before the worst. I have the feeling that the worst is far from over, even though my relief at seeing Fiona well and alive is infinite.

The facts are impossible to ignore though. Kelli's words. What does that mean? She's not a private detective? That explains why she would be able to call in help. It's a moot point at the moment, as we can't go anywhere. I want to know more, but that, too, will have to wait.

Pete and his friends were upstairs drinking after locking Fiona in the shelter. She sits next to me, her back straight against the wall. It looks like she expects to jump up and defend herself at any moment, even with me and Kelli here, even with Pete having his hands tied behind his back.

I want to pick up that rifle and make him tell the truth. That's just a fantasy though. I know Fiona suffers from mild claustrophobia, and I can't make things worse for her.

"I didn't touch her, I swear!" Pete speaks up as if reading my mind. Kelli is watching the scene carefully. Detective Kelli Jameson.

"You put a sack over my head and locked me in here!" she accuses.

"Because you killed Lucas!"

Outside, the storm is howling, horrible timing and somehow an ideal backdrop.

I wait for Fiona's denial. It never comes. Perhaps she thinks he isn't worth an answer.

"Why would you think that?" Kelli asks.

"Because I saw them come out of the shack, and there was blood on the wall!"

Fiona shrugs as if those accusations leave her unfazed. I know her better. She's trying not to panic.

I *know* her. She's not capable of killing anyone.

Not even if that person raped her friend? I wonder and instantly feel guilty. But that nagging voice won't shut up. *You* could do it if someone you love was hurt, couldn't you?

But they didn't want anything to do with Erica. While part of me was shocked, another tried to rationalize their behavior, telling myself that they were young, and traumatized by the mere concept of what had happened.

"That must have been so bad," Fiona snaps back at Pete. "Remember the last time we saw you coming out of a room? Erica was barely conscious. There was blood on the sheet."

"I didn't do anything!"

"But Lucas did," Kelli says. Her voice is calm, but she, too, is ghostly white. Or perhaps it's the lighting in here. Even though it's not cold, my skin feels chilled with the fear of what this exchange might unearth. I wish I could hold on to her.

Hide like I have for most of my life. I won't be able to hold back those tears much longer. For Erica, for Fiona and their friends, and for myself as well.

I can't leave George. I can't run away, but God, I wish I could.

"I'm not talking to you," he scoffs. "You're a cop? Figure it out. The real criminal is sitting right there. Erica wanted to party, and she cried wolf the next day."

"She didn't even know what was happening! God, you're disgusting," Fiona says. I close my eyes for a second, wishing I was somewhere else, someone else, where I didn't have to recognize the kind of knowledge these young girls have.

Then again, it's not so different from the way Ellen and I grew up, is it? It's just something we didn't talk about often, together, or with our friends. Underage drinking and parties aren't an invention of the current generation. And those who took advantage always existed as well.

What did they do? Why is he so adamant that they had something to do with Lucas's death? Denial?

Kelli is apparently asking herself the same questions.

"It looks like we're going to be here for a while. And I have to tell you, Pete, this is not an official interrogation. Nothing you tell me could be used in court, but perhaps it would help you to tell the truth. Your friend is already dead. You must be upset."

"Upset? You bet your ass I'm upset those bitches killed my friend."

"Pete, watch your mouth." I can't help it, even though I know it won't have much of an impact. I can't help thinking this is an unusual situation for all of us. Probably for the first time in his life, he's forced to listen to women. There is something satisfying about that—and about seeing him with his hands still behind his back.

"So what, Mrs. Burke, it's true. I saw them."

I can't hold back the gasp. Kelli seems less impressed, just continues the conversation as if this was perfectly normal. Fiona is wrapping her arms around herself. I gently touch her shoulder, still making her flinch.

"We'll get to that. First, tell me about what happened that night with Erica. Was it just coincidence that you became Lucas's alibi, or did he involve you in the plan from the start?"

"Plan, there was no plan! We had a few drinks. Erica kept coming on to Lucas. What did she expect?"

I can sense the anger radiating off of Fiona, or maybe it's me. This might not be official, but I can tell Kelli went into professional, detached mode. I've seen another side to her.

"Right, what could she expect at that moment, I'm interested in that myself. You really thought she was able to consent?"

I expect him to sneer at that, but to my surprise, he doesn't.

"She walked into the room, didn't she? But Lucas didn't expect to be shot."

"He would have done it again," Fiona says. "With no consequences as usual. What would happen next time? You wanted to kidnap a child just to see if you could get away with it? Murder someone?"

"You got far ahead of us, didn't you?"

I catch Kelli's gaze. We're both startled. This conversation has become oddly specific. Both Fiona and Pete stare at each other, a silent standoff, as if they're unaware of the witnesses to their exchange.

"We'd already seen the lists, and plans you made every time you were drinking down in your parents' party room, or Kyle's apartment. So stupid to keep them on your phone."

"What you saw was a video game."

"Erica is a real person! And Lexi's little sister is too."

"We were just joking! But you killed him. You murdered my best friend!"

I am more disturbed by the minute, but still amazed by his tears. The entitlement is mind-boggling.

Above all, I'm gripped by the growing fear that I, that everyone in town contributed to this by letting people like him go too far, seeing the behavior of families like his as something we had to accept. Maybe we didn't have to.

"I'm so sorry," I say to Fiona. The lights are starting to flicker, and a huge bang makes all of us jump.

"It was an accident," she says, her eyes filled with tears too. "I swear it was an accident, but I'm not sorry he's dead. He was a horrible person."

"Shut up," Pete yells.

We hear another crash, and then the sound of screeching metal.

Chapter Twenty-Three

Kelli

I couldn't care less about Bradley's crocodile tears, and even Fiona's obvious claustrophobia isn't at the front of my mind. I'm most worried about Merin who's sitting still and quietly, absorbing the troubling facts. Maybe I've taken this too far, maybe we would have never gotten here if it wasn't for the four of us trapped in a freaking tornado shelter.

We'll have to figure out the finer details, but a few things seem for certain.

Pete all but confessed that Erica was too drunk to consent, and Lucas forced himself on her anyway.

Fiona and her friends had a hand in Lucas's death.

I knew I hated this case when I first heard about it, and I haven't changed my mind since.

"I'm going to tell all of this to the sheriff," Pete threatens. "You're going away for life!"

"You're a moron! Once they see that plan of yours, the one that you and Lucas came up with together, it will be you who's going away! You really think they'll believe it's a video game? You had pictures of Lexi's sister, for Christ's sake!"

"Blasphemy and lies." He laughs. "You hear that, Detective Jameson? Are you going to arrest her too, or are you protecting your lover?" Pete laughs some more, bordering on insane. The lights have come back on, but it's still eerie.

"I wasn't kidding about the backup," I say. "And unlike Sheriff Cross and Officer LeBlanc, they won't be friends with your parents."

"So, you are covering for a murderer, because you're fucking her aunt?" Pete sneers.

"I'm not covering for anyone, and you better shut up now. Fiona will have to answer some questions, but from everything I've heard, I'm sure she'll come out of it much better than you will."

I'm not looking at Merin, rattled by the accusation. For a long uncomfortable time, everyone is silent. And then we hear something crashing outside, louder than before.

I wonder how reliable these shelters are. I never want to be near one again for the rest of my life.

⁂

I'm trying to think of a life beyond this confined space I'm sharing with a curious group of people: The married woman I'm attracted to and want to protect above all, her niece who might have had a hand in a rapist's death, and the rapist's best buddy.

Times to remember. Eventually, the noises from outside die down, but my thoughts are still loud.

What's going to happen next?

I notice Fiona has her hands folded. She's praying.

"So," I say, "I hear you get this kind of weather often around here." How did that come out of my mouth? Maybe I, too, could use a prayer, or anything to guide me on the right path.

Merin shoots me an incredulous look.

"Yes, sorry, that didn't come out right. I mean, you are pretty much used to this? You know what to do."

"We try the best we can," she says. "The rest is...hope. You never know where exactly it hits. Of course, politicians haven't done much to keep us safer."

"Figures," Pete sneers. "I have to be stuck with a murderer and a couple of dykes, and now you want to tell me about that climate change shit? We have tornadoes every freaking year."

It's inappropriate at the moment, but his predictable summary of the events makes me want to laugh. That's a lot of talking points in a couple of sentences.

"Don't listen to him," I say. "We'll figure out all of this once we can get out of here."

<hr/>

First things first. Fiona and Merin climb out, and I watch Pete as I follow. The air feels a lot different now, and not just because of all those revelations that have been made.

"I'll tell the sheriff you held me in here," Pete threatens.

Merin who is on the phone with Ellen, shoots him an annoyed gaze.

"Try to explain to the sheriff that you kidnapped my niece."

I, too, make a call.

"How are you doing? I hear it's been pretty bad down there."

"I'm fine. Happened to be within steps of a tornado shelter. What's the ETA on the backup? We have quite a situation here."

"I'd say. They're on their way, but they'll have to see what the roads look like."

"Sure. Thanks. I'll call you later."

I'd prefer if they were at the police station by the time we arrive there, but that's probably wishful thinking.

I'll have to stand my ground. They can't do anything to Fiona until they have sorted out the kidnapping. Besides, I'm sure they'll be busy. As I look around, I become aware of all the shrubs, branches, and debris around. It's more than I expected, but the Bradleys' mansion stood firm, no surprise there. Perhaps it wasn't that bad after all? People are told to seek shelter as a precaution, because, as Merin said, you never know.

"Backup is on the way," I tell her. "Let's get the car and bring Fiona home first."

"You're just going to drive me around like this?" Pete whines. "That can't be legal?"

"Oh, would you shut up? You kidnapped a minor and lied in court, for starters. You want me to come up with more reasons to detain you? Like you knew about your brother selling drugs to teens?" For a moment, I think he's going to stick out his tongue at me. Kids, all right. He shuts up at that.

I, too, am a tad speechless when I see my car, still standing, but almost camouflaged by branches that might have come from the Bradleys' backyard and elsewhere, and a piece of siding. A window in the back is cracked. Another one this time. My insurance will have a field day.

This can't go on much longer. I need to get Fiona and Merin home.

Fiona helps me clear the car while Merin watches a brooding Pete Bradley. I have Fiona get into the front passenger seat, Pete in the back. Before Merin and I get in as well, I hold her back. There are tears in her eyes.

"Everything okay at your sister's? She must be happy we're bringing Fiona home safely." I keep an eye on the teenagers, but they don't communicate at all, each staring into different directions.

"No one was hurt badly," she says. "That's good."

I remember that when we left, the sheriff was there. So was George. "What happened?"

"Storm blew the roof off their house."

"Wow. I'm so sorry."

I'm out of my depth. I'm not sure about their situation when it comes to finances, insurance, and such. But in a small town, a community comes together for their own? I guess that depends on whether they consider them one of their own. They should?

"They'll fix it. It's just been a lot."

"I understand. Let's get Fiona home first, okay?"

She nods before she opens the door and sits next to Pete in the backseat.

It takes me a couple of attempts, but the car starts, and we can leave. I can't hold back the words, "Thank God."

<hr>

My relief is a bit short-lived when the drive takes longer and longer. All occupants of my car are silent, staring out at the destructive path the tornado has taken. Ellen's home is not the only one that has suffered substantial damage. I've seen pictures like this on TV, but not in real life.

I must stay focused.

We finally make it to the Collins' home. I have barely hit the brakes when Fiona opens the door and runs towards the house where Ellen and her husband are standing outside. They hug their daughter closely. I can see George, and Officer Woodward.

I have to deliver Bradley first, though I feel bad leaving them here. I get out of the car with her.

Merin turns to me. I think of all the witnesses. I don't care, just pull her into a close embrace.

"What can I do to help? Do they have somewhere to stay? Someone will have to come in and look at the structure, I assume. If I can do anything…"

She leans into me for a few seconds, then straightens and looks past me at Pete who is sneering back at us.

"Make sure he doesn't get away with what he did. We can figure out the rest."

"I promise," I say, then head back to the car while she goes to join her family.

Pete laughs when I get back into the driver's seat.

"That's pathetic," he says.

I don't deign to comment. The sooner I can get rid of him and talk to some real cops, the sooner I can get back to Merin. I've made up my mind. I'm not going to leave until we have Fiona's situation figured out. That's the only way I can really help them.

I'm not going to lie, the events of the past few hours have shaken me. I've seen big storms on the coast, and flooding, but there are parts out here that look like a war zone. Closer to town, it's a little better but still a lot of roads are blocked. I hope that the cavalry my boss sent in has made it here.

"You're never going to prove it," Pete says. "Fiona kept coming on to me the way Erica did with Lucas."

"Keep talking," I say mildly.

"It's not fair," he rages. "All he wanted was a bit of fun, and they killed him for it."

"If I was you, I'd be careful with those accusations. The Collins' could sue you for that too. And I'm sure it wasn't Fiona's idea to put a sack over her head."

He's actually pouting. I'm so sick and tired of this.

"How about for once in your life, you take responsibility?"

164

I don't expect him to agree with me, but it feels good to say it out loud.

Chapter
Twenty-Four

Merin

U pon closer examination, it's part of the roof that's missing, which is bad enough. Ellen and Drew have secured the place best they could, and they'll spend the night at a friend's outside of town, whose house hasn't suffered damage. Drew has already called some friends and family. They will clean up things as much as possible. In the next few days, carpenters and electricians will make a killing.

I shiver, hard, aware that I haven't slept or eaten in a while.

But we have Fiona back.

For how long? The nagging voice keeps asking. Given the staggering relief we all feel, I can't bring myself to raise the questions yet. What exactly happened the night Lucas died, and who pulled the trigger?

It seems like an alternate reality, those confessions made in the shelter.

Pete covered for Lucas. No surprise there.

Fiona and her friends accidentally killed Lucas.

"Are you okay?" George puts a hand on the center of my back. "You went really pale there for a moment."

"I'm fine," I say, even though it's a blatant lie. I didn't get to make a revelation. That doesn't mean it's not the truth. But I'll have to stay. My life is here. My family. I might die here. That realization nearly breaks my composure, but I need to keep it together, for the people I care about. "I think I just need something to eat. Coffee. Have you been back to the house yet? Any idea how bad it might be?"

Please, God, let us have a roof. I can deal with a few broken windows or loose shingles.

"I don't know. But we should all take a break. This will take a while. We can check on the house meanwhile."

"Yes, let's do that."

We're in the car a moment later, and it's not even as awkward as I've feared. If anything, Fiona's story—which he doesn't know yet—and the storm remind us that there are bigger things than our own fears. If he wants to see that man, Liam, if he makes him happy, who am I to disagree?

Great, now I have that song in my head. I try to focus. Kelli didn't tell the whole truth either, but at least she had a good reason, a job to do. Detective Jameson. Could I do that, visit her at her parents' B&B, lean on her for guidance...about what? How to come out? I don't want to keep leaning on her.

It's something else that I want.

I have a small window for the fantasy, about what I could do or where I could go, when it all comes crashing down on me.

Like the pile of debris that used to be our house. The home that I said I couldn't leave. With a beautiful view and so many memories.

Have I brought this on us because in the past few days, I have cursed our home?

For long moments, I don't feel anything. I walk closer, confused, in disbelief. This can't be the house I left yesterday?

If I don't panic, does it mean I got this, we can figure this out, start over?

The next moment, I'm on my knees, sobbing, because no matter what I think or do, start over is what we'll have to do. There is nothing left to save.

"Merin." I can hear it in his voice that he's crying too. Is it because our marriage crumbled as well under pressure? I don't know.

Kelli

At the police station, they have power, and fortunately, coffee. I join the backup sent by the chief, a couple of detectives from the county, and a guy from Internal Affairs. He has cleared one of the offices for us.

Pete is finally back behind bars, but we have no time to waste. His lawyer will be here soon.

"We have bagels too," the female detective says, and it's only then that I realize it's been longer since Merin and I left Ellen's than I thought. "Help yourself. We have a lot to talk about."

"No kidding. Let's start with Pete Bradley since his lawyer is on the way. He lied about the rape. Erica McQuade was unable to consent. He was a witness to the crime and..." I take a look at the glass behind me. "The sheriff isn't here yet?"

"One of our colleagues is with him right now," she says, "but there's been some damage in town, so they haven't made it here yet."

Fair enough. I nod. "I can't say to what extent he's involved, but apparently Bradley's younger brother Adam dealt in school. They threatened Fiona Collins multiple times, and Officer LeBlanc and his partner tried to halt the investigation."

She raises an eyebrow. "How?"

I describe what happened that night, grateful for the coffee but still antsy. There is too much to do in too little time. It's a miracle they're even here already. Half of the town is without power, and I'm still worried that it might help the same people to get off.

"Pete Bradley is at the center of all of this."

"He also claims that Fiona Collins shot Lucas Gavin?"

"That's not at all clear yet. He kidnapped Fiona and locked her in the shelter where we found her, but then the storm hit, and we had to stay. Fiona says it was an accident. I was going to interview her, but I thought it was more important to reunite her with her family first."

At least it doesn't sound one bit defensive. The other detectives have seen the damage around here.

"They're missing a roof," I add. "I don't think they're going anywhere, so I'm sure this can wait. Bradley on the other hand was involved in multiple crimes, and I overheard him saying to Fiona that, I quote, the same that happened to Erica might happen to her."

I hope what I'm saying makes sense to them because it sounds chaotic to me. That's what I found here: Chaos. On so many levels.

"Anyway, I haven't even been back to my hotel yet. I hope it's still standing. Is there any chance we could continue this tomorrow?"

She looks a bit surprised.

"What?"

"We will definitely have to talk again in the coming days. I thought you'd cleared it with the chief—we'll take it from here. Thank you so much for your help, Detective Jameson."

"You're...welcome, I guess."

I knew that moment would come. I didn't think it would come so soon.

"What about Sheriff Cross?" I ask.

"I think they need every hand right now, but with what you told us, we have a lot to look at in this department," the Internal Affairs investigator says.

"Take the afternoon," the detective says. "Just don't turn off your phone."

It all feels kind of anti-climactic, but I don't have much time to indulge in my feelings. My first stop is back at the Collins'. Drew is still outside with some of his friends. Truth be told, it doesn't look like they made much progress.

"We were lucky," he tells me, sounding relieved, nonetheless. "No gas leak. Aside from the roof, it could be worse."

I look up to the area where the storm left a gaping hole. I'm not sure if it's sarcasm, or if he actually means it.

"I'm sorry, but I'll still have to talk to Fiona. I wanted to make sure that she's okay...considering."

"Considering Bradley put a sack over her head and locked her in the shelter?"

This time, the sentiment is unmistakable.

"I know. He's not going to get away this time. I swear. Can I talk to her?"

"She's over at Merin and George's." He sighs. "They have it worse."

My stomach lurches at his matter-of-fact delivery.

"Worse? How?"

"You'll see when you get there. I offered to take them to my friend's house as well. They don't mind. But Merin didn't want to leave yet."

"I don't understand."

"It's gone," he says, now with a hint of impatience. "Their house is gone."

I have no more words. This damn case. This damn town. But there's somewhere I need to be right now.

☙

I want to help. I want it so badly, but today, I seem to be the third wheel wherever I go.

"Don't do anything crazy!" George warns her. "It's not safe."

Merin looks like she wants to argue, but there's nothing much for her to say.

"You talk to her," he says to me, as if giving up. "We made sure nothing's going to blow up in there...but other than that, there's not much we can do. Look at this. What is she hoping to find? We'll have to get some equipment to clear this away."

"Your...papers?"

I can't even begin to imagine a situation like this. I step closer to Merin, unsure if she even realizes I'm here. Or if she wants me here at all.

"We had the important stuff in the shelter," he says. "Every-thing else..." No explanation needed.

Abruptly, she turns around and I wrap my arms around her.

"Hey. I know this looks bad."

"No but," Merin mumbles against my shoulder. "There's no freaking but. Don't try."

"I wasn't going to." I was, but that's irrelevant at the moment.

"Look...if you don't want to go to Ellen and Drew's friend, how about you come with me to my hotel? I called earlier. The power was out for a few hours, but other than that they seem okay. You could get something to eat. They'll have a room for you too."

"I don't know."

"You can't stay here." Over her shoulder, I receive an encouraging nod from George. "Look, Drew told me Fiona is here? I need to steal her for a moment. Why don't you and George go and wait for me at the hotel?"

It's not my first choice to spend the evening with both of them, but given the circumstances, we can't be too picky. And they are without a doubt the kindest people in this place.

George has Liam.

Merin has options that I will provide for her. We'll see where that gets us.

Without any argument, Fiona sits next to me in the car.

"There's a detective that will come see you soon," I say. "You'll be okay. Just make sure you tell them what you told me. It was an accident."

She nods but doesn't look at me. She's probably still shell-shocked, for many reasons.

"I imagine Lucas came there to threaten you, like Pete did before. Maybe it was about Erica, maybe about the money Pete's brother claimed you owed him. You were scared."

"I guess."

"Lucas brought the gun I assume." I'm aware I'm walking a fine line here, but this town has already taken too much from the girls, and their families. I want to help any way I can, but for that, I need the truth. Fiona stays silent. That's what I was afraid of.

"Please, let me help you. I know you didn't mean to kill anyone. And we don't want this to take away from his guilt, or Pete's."

"Lexi brought the gun," she says. "After...Erica, we tried to stay close to them. To find evidence, you know?"

Okay, this is more than I expected, but it makes a whole lot more sense than what everyone of us thought we knew.

"That could have been dangerous."

I deserved that patient gaze she's giving me.

"Anyway, we found something on Lucas's phone, but we didn't get a copy." Anger has made the color drain from her face. "They were texting, congratulating each other, discussing what they could do next. Kidnap a child for ransom? They had pictures of Lexi's little sister. I don't know, maybe Kyle still has them."

"You were going to confront him? Maybe scare him a little?"

Fiona shakes her head.

"You know, we saw Erica after...and we knew the stories of their parents, and what they got away with. The sheriff and most of his officers won't touch them."

"That will change now."

"Will it? I'm not so sure. Anyway, we knew that if we didn't do anything, this would go on and on. But most of all, we wanted to do it for Erica."

I want to leave the car, but I can't. I can't let her or Merin—or Erica McQuade—down.

"I didn't lie to you," she says with a sigh. "I'm really grateful to you for saving me twice. Amanda, Lexi and I...We met many times. We talked about it."

"You cut ties with Erica so she wouldn't have to lie if anyone asked her questions."

Finally, it all makes sense in a tragic way.

"It was hard," Fiona admits. "I hate that she thinks we let her down, but we believed we were doing the right thing. I still believe it. Whatever happens from now on, she'll have nothing to do with it."

"What happened?" I keep my voice low.

"We aren't as brave as we thought we were, taking out the bad guy and all. He got mad and went for the gun. We all tried to wrestle it from him, and it went off."

"What did you do after that?"

"We panicked. Nothing had gone as we imagined it, and we...We wrapped him in a blanket and carried him to the lake not far away." Fiona shudders. "He was so heavy."

"You were in shock. You just have to stick to the same story. It's the truth—right?"

"Of course. Do you think I'll go to prison?" she asks, too calm for my liking. Shock. For certain.

"I'll do my best to make sure it won't happen. Everyone will know that the sheriff and some of the officers routinely covered for the Gavins and the Bradleys. Pete kidnapped you. You were afraid for your lives and the life of Lexi's sister. It will be okay."

Fiona shakes her head with a bitter laugh.

"Nothing will ever be okay. I can't even imagine what it was like for Erica in that room, and I didn't even come close. You probably think I'm a bad person, but I'm not sad he's dead. He did horrible things too."

"I'm not going to tell you how to feel," I say. "I will drop you off at your parents'. I know things are tricky right now, but I recommend you get a lawyer soon. Remember, it was an accident. You had reason to confront him, it got out of hand."

To my surprise, she leans over and hugs me hard.

"Thank you," she whispers.

I wish I could do more to alleviate the trauma they have experienced. Seeing some accountability might go a long way though.

Chapter
Twenty-Five

Merin

We have some food and tea at the hotel restaurant, Kelli, George and I. I can barely taste anything, and even though it's not cold in here, I keep shivering.

It's not like I can complain much, under the circumstances, because Kelli took care of everything. We have a roof over our heads tonight, food, insurance and other papers. The latter isn't luck. Those of us who have grown up here, and that's pretty much everyone in town, know what to do.

But nothing, no one prepared us for this day. My family has been mostly spared. An uncle of mine once had to rebuild. We never thought it would happen to us...My throat goes tight again.

"Excuse me for a moment?"

George gets up to make a phone call, Kelli casting a thoughtful glance after him. Yes, I know he's going to call Liam. I can't comment on that now.

It's only now that I realize I put on the bracelet earlier. Her gift to me. The reminder. I'm ridiculously happy to have it, as if her offer didn't stand without it. I got to save something.

"I know you have a lot to consider," she says. "I'll be here for a few more days, to consult with the team."

"Detective Jameson."

"I'm so sorry I couldn't tell you the whole truth. My boss does know the Gavins, though I don't think he's seen them much in recent years. I can't believe he knows much about their behavior...Most of my assignment was about the sheriff and his gang."

"Liz didn't know about it, did she?"

"Very little if anything at all. She was never the main target."

"Okay." She seems to be waiting for more, but I don't know what that would be. I don't know what I could possibly give her. When I stay silent, Kelli picks up the conversation again.

"After you've taken care of...everything you need to take care of, whether you'd like to go somewhere else or just get away for a bit, please, call me."

"You're going to help me with my coming-out?"

"I'm going to help you with anything you need."

I know she's sincere. Somehow that makes things worse. I don't want to be someone who needs help.

I want to be *wanted*. I'm exhausted, and everything material I've ever held dear is gone—except for that bracelet.

"That's very kind of you, but nothing has changed. People here need me, even more than before."

"I get it." I have the impression she wants to say more, but George returns to the table that moment.

"Kelli, thank you so much for everything. But I guess we should call it a night?"

I know that today of all days he doesn't mean to be patronizing. It still feels that way to me.

Even though we have shared a bed for nearly two decades, for better or worse, the room feels small and claustrophobic. I think of the shelter, all that has been said. I didn't know.

As I sit on the side of the bed, I can't even cry any more, I'm so exhausted.

I can't leave. There's so much to do, to think about.

Who cares about what I want?

"How is he?" I ask. "Liam, is he okay?"

"It wasn't so bad where he lives," George says.

"Good." Silence again. I'm tired of this too.

"Merin, I'm really sorry about all this." He sits next to me and lays a hand on my shoulder.

"It's not your fault that Lucas Gavin raped Erica, or that the girls got their hands on a gun. And unlike some, I don't believe that gay people can make natural disasters happen."

He smiles but winces a little. We rarely say it out loud. Gay. Lesbian. The world should be more open, kinder, these days, but so often, it's the opposite. Sometimes it's hard not to fall for the lure of prejudice: As long as you're silent, you can be one of us. It's a treacherous comfort. It still hurts—us, and others.

Then again, beggars can't be choosers, right? We don't have anywhere to go. We depend on the kindness of our neighbors, prejudiced or not.

"We'll have to take it day by day," he says. "Get the place cleaned up, see what the insurance can do. I'll always support you, you know that."

That sounds ominous. Perhaps everything that has happened made me paranoid, or perhaps I can blame that on Kelli. It was bound to happen when we got closer. She was never able to see a good thing here in the first place. Now I seem to look at the people the same way.

Will I ever be able to go back?

"What do you mean?" I ask.

"What I said. You should get some sleep."

I repeat to myself what I said to Kelli. People here need me. Of course, I'll do the responsible thing. George and I will find a new place to live. Life will go on. The rest will be nothing but a fantasy—like the idea that I could just go next door and be with her. Like the idea that I would ever leave.

Chapter Twenty-Six

Kelli

P ete Bradley will be held accountable this time—relatively speaking. His big shot lawyers will still argue that this "kid with a bright future" made a mistake he shouldn't pay for his whole life. At least the girls will be able to get out of this relatively unscathed. I heard their questioning went as well as they could have expected, given the circumstances. I hope they'll be able to repair their relationship with Erica.

So much destruction. As I'm packing up, I have to admit I overestimated myself greatly. First, when I thought this would be an unpleasant, but quick affair. Then, when I thought I could help real change along.

Money will still talk in this town, even if to a lesser extent.

Some people will still feel the need to hide deep in the closet in order to avoid prejudice and persecution. I didn't save anyone, really. The women around here do what they need to do to protect themselves. At least, this time around, they're not the only ones who pay the price.

The corruption in the police department will be rooted out, and Liz Woodward might be the only one keeping her job.

My job is done.

ㅇ◦○◦○

Four days later, my last day in town, I ask Merin to come see me one more time, for dinner in a restaurant out of town—a public place, but far away enough not to make things too awkward.

She says yes. *Figures*. She's probably relieved to see me go.

"Did you figure everything out with the insurance company?"

That was not the first thing I meant to ask her.

"Yes, we did," she says as she fastens her seatbelt. "It's a mess...and I guess I'm still in shock. I've been wearing my sister's clothes for the past few days. We've had meals from people who aren't much better off, but everyone's helping."

"Good. About that."

"Please, don't make it weird. There's a number where you can donate if you like."

I reach into my pocket and produce the check anyway.

"Please, don't say no. I know the insurance will come through eventually, and you'll do what you have to do. I wasn't able to lure you out of this place, and you wouldn't have a passionate affair with me, so...*please*, just take this?"

"Kelli."

"Don't cry. It's not that much."

She holds the piece of paper in her hand, regarding it for a few seconds.

"I wish I was that proud, but I don't think I am. Thank you."

"You've been carrying a lot. And again, it's too small a number for misplaced pride."

To my relief, she laughs. "Thank you so much." She leans in for a hug which I'm willing to give...but somehow her lips end up on mine, a promise that can never come true but feels incredibly sweet, nonetheless.

Chapter Twenty-Seven

Merin

I am a coward. I want to be with her so much, not just tonight. I want to get to know the woman behind the undercover assignment, want to be with her in an environment where we both can be comfortable.

It's never going to happen, because...I said it. It's all me.

Kelli pays for dinner, coffee and dessert, and a little nightcap in another bar. She's not drinking.

"I'm sorry," I say. "We could have just gone to the diner. I think people have other problems now than to gossip."

"That's okay. I wanted to take you out one last time."

One last time. I feel hollow except for that lingering omnipresent fear. I thought having some closure for Fiona and Ellen would change that, but it's the worst it's ever been—and not all of it stems from the storm's aftermath. In town, things aren't so bad. Most businesses have survived, and owners are busy repairing the damage.

"That place you described, your parents' hotel by the sea, it sounded nice."

"It's real," she says softly.

Not for me, it is not.

"No pressure." Kelli takes my hand on the table. "But don't throw out my number yet, okay?"

"I won't," I promise.

⁓

Just like that, she's gone, and people are slowly getting over what was the real reason for her stay. Aside from Liz Woodward and a couple of others, there's all new staff at the police station. The judge who let Lucas Gavin off has retired suddenly.

George and I have moved into an apartment to figure out what comes next. It's still sparsely furnished, but we were able to have family over for the first time.

"It wasn't so bad," I muse when I close the door behind the last guest. "Everyone had a place to sit."

"Yeah."

He's awfully silent all of a sudden. We used to be better at that, be comfortable in each other's presence, convinced that we were doing the right thing. We inspire youth, right? We help them on the right path. Except it feels like it's been a long time since I've done any of it. Inspire. Help. Maybe I'm the one who needs help, still. I haven't cashed in that check yet.

George starts clearing the dessert dishes and wine glasses from the table. I flinch at the sound the plates make when he sets them down.

"Merin, we need to talk," he says.

Did he find out about the check? How? I've carried it on me since that night.

"About what?"

"Isn't that obvious? Us?"

I'm still not sure what to make of it, or what's different from a few weeks or years ago. We both sit on opposite sides at the table.

"I've been thinking a lot...Since we lost the house," he says. "I'm sure you have too. We were lucky no one was injured that day. We could have lost so much more."

"But we didn't. And we're here, we have a roof over our heads, we still have our jobs...What are you saying?"

"I've been hiding my whole life." Finally, he meets my gaze. "You are my best friend, Merin, and you have helped me so much, but aren't you tired of it all? Always those little white lies, to make people comfortable who don't deserve it?"

Why is he talking like Kelli all of a sudden?

"Who says they don't deserve it? They're our family and friends."

"I'm not sure anymore if they care, or if they ever did. But that's their problem. It can all be over in a heartbeat! Liam asked me to marry him."

My jaw drops. I am speechless. This is not something I expected to happen, ever.

"After all these years? Why now?"

"Because he feels the same. We don't want to waste any more time."

I'm on my feet in a heartbeat.

"So all this time with me, it was wasted? You spent this many years looking for an out?"

"That's not what I said." His calm tone makes everything worse. "It made sense at the time, and we both agreed to it."

"How is this going to work? With the school? You want a divorce?" My voice goes up a notch at the last word. The elephant in the room. The word that changes everything. I'm no longer safe in my denial.

"I'll figure things out with the school. Worst case scenario, I'd sue them. We already had some national news coverage because of Lucas Gavin. I'm not scared, not anymore."

I hold my head in my hands. "What am I going to do?"

He reaches out to gently pull my hands away. "Don't do this. Merin, you are the strongest person I know. I can't ever pay back what you did for me, but honestly, life is too short. Yours, mine, I know we still have so much to do and to give."

It's so strange, almost like tragedy has energized him, while it did the opposite to me. I've been feeling exhausted, lost, for a long time. Useless.

"I'm not going to stand in your way," I say. "I'll sign whatever you want me to."

"Thank you, Merin. You know what, let's do those dishes tomorrow." He gets a couple of new glasses out of the cabinet and pours a glass of wine for each of us. "How about we celebrate freedom?"

I stare at the glass he's handing me for almost a full minute.

Then I shake my head. "I can't. I'm sorry, I can't."

I pick up my keys and coat and leave.

Not many businesses are open at this hour. I used to think of this as a feature of a cozy sleepy town. Safe.

It wasn't safe for a lot of people. Sure, things are better now, but what is going to happen when George and I announce our separation to the world? When he tells everyone that he's with Liam now?

I end up in the bar where I first saw Kelli. She didn't notice me, at least I don't think so. But I saw her the moment she came in, back straight, confident. It's not George's fault, not directly, but he destroyed every hope I had of trying to make this different life come true. If I called her now, she'd never believe I'm doing it for us. It would look like I did it for a lack of options, and isn't that right?

Except...I wanted to. But that doesn't matter anymore. I've told her many times that I couldn't make that choice, until she offered to be friends only. God, I could use a real friend, and so much more. At least the people I care about will be happy.

George and his husband.

Kelli and the new woman by her side she'll have no trouble finding.

By the time Thanksgiving comes around, George has already moved out. He's still in negotiations with the school, and as expected, it didn't go so well. I don't know much more when I arrive at Ellen's. I dreaded this day. It's a big party, with our parents, some aunts and uncles and friends. On the bright side, if I'm lucky it will be so busy, I might be able to avoid any painful conversations.

I told Mom and Dad I didn't want to talk about it and avoided picking up the phone altogether. Here I am with a bowl of homemade cranberry sauce, making a peace offer.

Eat this. Leave me alone.

"Mrs. Burke, hi. Happy Thanksgiving."

I turn around to come face to face with Erica McQuade.

"Erica, it's good to see you. How are you?"

"Happy to be here," she says. "I don't know if Fiona told you, but we had a long talk. My parents are going to move away, so I'm changing schools."

"Best of luck."

"Thank you."

If she can be out and about, doing friendly small talk, I have no excuse, do I?

I still end up in the kitchen with my glass of wine. It's all I can do not to panic. Any time now, someone's going to ask about George. And once they do, a lot of questions will follow. Did I know? If I did, why did I cover for him?

Did he do the same for me?

It's where Mom and Ellen find me, well on my way to getting drunk.

"I am so sorry, honey," Mom says as she sits at the table with me. "You deserved better."

Funny, Kelli said something similar. But Kelli understood something about me I wasn't even sure of myself. Something that has no place here. Does it?

"I agree," Ellen says. "What was he thinking, doing all of this so publicly? Didn't he think of your reputation?"

Part of me agrees. Another, a lot less polite one, is threatening to break free.

"I don't know if that's the right question. He's gay. He's in love." I didn't miss the look she and Mom exchange. "I'll survive."

"So, the school is okay with this, you both still working there?"

"We are getting a divorce. No one killed anyone." The words are out of my mouth before I can stop myself. "That's not what I meant. Come on. People are making such a big deal of it."

"Because it is! How can you trust anyone anymore? He's working with young kids that are easily influenced."

"I can't believe this. You believe that crap?"

"Girls," Mom scolds the two of us. "It's Thanksgiving."

"Yeah, but I'm not really that thankful at the moment," I snap and get up to leave the room. On second thought, I refill my glass and take it with me.

I breathe a bit easier, outside, alone again, on the porch. You see, Kelli? I knew all of this would happen. I had my whole life to draw that conclusion. There's no comfort in being right.

"You really liked her, didn't you?"

The peaceful solitude didn't last long. At least it's Fiona.

"It's not always about that."

"You didn't love George?" she asks.

I'm not sure I can trust my voice. I'm still too close to tears for comfort. "He's a great guy," I finally say. "I could always talk to him about everything. It's not easy to find friends like that."

"True," she acknowledges. "But you were married, and now he's going to marry a guy. I thought you and Kelli might—"

"No," I interrupt her.

"Why not?"

My vision is already blurring.

"You know what people are saying." So what? I don't want them to say the same things about me? "It's not as easy as that."

"It helps to tell the truth, even if it's just to one person," she says, leaving me wondering. "Everyone deserves to be happy." After a spontaneous hug, she goes back inside.

Questions. Truths. Coward. I pick up the glass and empty it in one swallow.

⁘

I call a cab for myself and only say goodbye when the driver honks outside.

"Let me get you some leftovers," Ellen calls after me. I shake my head and walk faster. I need to get out of here. I need to do something, to stop blaming everyone else for my sins of omissions.

In the car, I call George, but only reach the voicemail. He's having Thanksgiving dinner with Liam and his parents.

"Are you okay, lady?" the driver asks.

"My house was destroyed in a tornado," I say, as if a total stranger is interested in this.

"Damn, that sucks. My brother was on his way home, broke both his legs. He's still in physical therapy."

"I'm so sorry."

What if George was right?

And Kelli?

I think of the kisses we shared, the night we spent together. A beautiful fantasy. But at one time, it was real, as real as George's relationship with Liam. I used to think I could inspire.

What is left of that?

Chapter Twenty-Eight

Kelli

I am up before dawn, taking a long walk on the beach. Sam, my parents' ten-year-old Golden Retriever, is with me. I love being by the sea, how healing it is. One day, I'll have to let go of false hopes, but until then, I'll cherish the memory.

I don't have anything to complain about—I have my apartment in the city and a place here on the beach I can always come to. My parents are well and alive, and they never forced me to make impossible choices to please the neighbors.

I still have a job.

But I can't stop thinking about her. That one night when I knew nothing was ever going to happen, but I dreamed about it, about her.

Every once in a while, I have nightmares, too, about three young men plotting the rape of a teenager, then, the kidnapping of a child. Teenage girls scared for their lives who felt they needed to pick up a rifle to defend themselves, the endless tragedy of it all.

Merin.

I hope there's healing for those girls, for Merin, for everyone who was impacted by the incredible bigotry and entitlement.

Sam and I walk back up to the house to a dramatic sunrise, the lighthouse in the distance. All of this is blessedly familiar. I can't fault Merin for choosing the familiar, and perhaps she is happier with her family, friends, and the secret than she could ever be with me. I have to return to the city, and work, in a few days.

Perhaps I should go on a date sometime, with a woman who isn't married...I already know that will take me a while. A part of me is still angry at her, maybe, but mostly at the people who created these claustrophobic circumstances for her.

My parents are already up and working to provide breakfast for their guests. They didn't close on Thanksgiving, instead offered a dinner menu for the patrons. A couple of people came for job-related reasons that they couldn't postpone. Now I wonder if some of them chose this place because they weren't welcome at their family's table.

Bigotry is bad, coddling bigotry is worse.

I look back at the horizon, trying to chase the dark thoughts as I crouch down to pet Sam.

"You love the beach too, huh? I guess we need to give you a bath."

"I can do that."

I look up to see my dad standing in front of me. Sam greets him with enthusiasm, as if he hasn't seen him forty minutes or so ago. The dignified enthusiasm of his age, but still. It makes me smile. I wish it was that easy to love, without prejudice, for humans as well.

"Oh no, I have time. I'll get breakfast after."

"There's a young lady here for you, Kelli."

I can sense the gentle curiosity. I can't help him much, because my heartbeat just went into overdrive.

"Um...okay."

It can't be. There was no call, no warning.

"Her name is Merin?"

"Yes. Thank you. I'll go."

I hasten my steps, almost jogging by the time I reach the front door. I walk down the corridor to the breakfast room where I see her. She's talking to my mom, a small suitcase standing next to her. What does that mean? She finally took me up on that offer, to have a bit of a time-out? Why didn't she call me?

"Merin."

They both turn to me. Mom smiles brightly. "Like I said, your room will be done soon. Please, take your time and have breakfast. This one's on the house. Enjoy your stay."

She pats my back before she leaves to talk to another guest who is trying to figure out the coffee machine.

Everything falls away.

"You're here." It's only a day after Thanksgiving, but it's almost a Christmas miracle. I'm definitely grateful.

"Yes." Merin hesitates. "Your parents are very nice."

"They are. But tell me...No, it's okay, like Mom said, take your time. I'm so glad to see you."

I draw her into an embrace. No one bats an eye, the occupants of the room too busy focusing on coffee, eggs, and bacon.

"Me too," she whispers, and I can tell from her tone that not everything is perfect. There's time to figure it out. I'll make good on my promise, even if that means I'll return to my day job later than planned. There's one thing I have to check though.

"Is Fiona okay?"

"She's great. She and Erica are making plans for college. We are so grateful you helped us."

"I wish I could have done more, but I'm glad they are talking. Come, let's get something to eat and sit?"

It's like a beautiful illusion, to have her here, hold her in my arms. I need something mundane like food and coffee, to lose the feeling that she might disappear again.

"I'd love to," she says.

A few minutes later we sit across from each other at a table by the window. We can see the water and the lighthouse from here.

I'm hungry, she must be too, but I can't help myself and take her hand.

Merin smiles wistfully. "I have a few days at least. I was hoping you might have time to show me around."

"Of course." I'm not sure what else to say. I don't want to rush her. Us. Whatever "us" can mean.

I want to ask so many questions. It's not the time.

"You must think I'm crazy, showing up here out of the blue."

"Not so much. I kept telling you that you should."

Merin glances at the panoramic view outside the window before she turns her gaze back to me.

"I know what you've been hoping for. And I didn't contact you because I didn't think it was something I could give to you. I didn't want to raise false hopes...for you and me. I'm afraid that hasn't changed. Things are complicated right now."

"You don't have to tell me."

"But I want to. George asked me for a divorce. Something about you live only once, not that I can blame him. If I thought the house coming down was the worst thing that could happen, well, it's all relative."

"I'm so sorry. He didn't leave you to deal with the insurance and all of that?"

"No, he would never do that. We neatly wrapped up all the paperwork before he and Liam moved to San Francisco."

That is a lot of new information, and I struggle to catch up, or keep my emotions in check.

"I lied," she says, her eyes welling up. Merin picks up a napkin and wipes her face in a quick angry gesture. "I didn't come for a vacation, I came because I have nowhere to go...other than live with George and Liam, maybe."

Sometimes, being right is a terrible thing. I wait, listen, even though the questions multiply in my mind.

"Fiona is the only person in my family talking to me at the moment. Everyone else needs...time. How is that even possible? I'm the same person!"

"Yes, you are." I do, and I have always felt boundless rage at people's self-serving prejudice, but I'm aware that doesn't help her right now.

"I hate coming to you like this," she says emphatically. "I don't expect you to take care of me, or anything. I just needed a bit of a different reality, you know?"

"I'm sorry to interrupt." Mom has fixed the problem the other guest had with the coffeemaker. "I couldn't help but overhear what you said. It might be none of my business, but let's make it clear, this is reality. You are welcome here. Stay as long as you need."

"Thank you, Mrs. Jameson."

I'm grateful for my mother being able to use words where I'd rather punch someone.

"It's true. We'll find a way. And I'm sure they'll come around."

Merin's smile tells me she appreciates the effort even though she's not sure they will.

⌘

One evening before dinner, while Merin's getting ready in her room, Mom sits down at the table with me. I know she has questions. Not all the answers are mine to give, and it's good to know that she'll respect the boundaries, Merin's, mine. We sit in companionable silence for a while.

"Your friend is going to stay for a bit."

That's not a question.

I nod. "If you need a payment in advance for the room, I can give it to you."

"Don't be ridiculous, we love having her here, and Sam's smitten. I don't want to be nosy, but I was wondering if she's going to move in with you."

The surprised laugh is all I can give her in reaction.

"I'm not sure if that's an option."

"Why not? She's obviously in love with you. Aren't you...?"

"It's complicated," I say, even though all I want is to know more. *Obviously?* Maybe she's right, but no matter how much I want it to be true, Merin is still in a vulnerable state. It wouldn't be fair to take advantage.

"And none of my business, I get it. Let me just say this. It's a shame when so-called family and friends behave that way."

I can't argue.

"There's no excuse for stopping to love your child like that. Unless they murdered someone in cold blood, then I would reconsider."

"Thanks. I think you're safe."

I think of the last time I saw Mrs. Gavin, for a few minutes without her husband.

"At first, I couldn't believe it, but he did that to the girl. He was never sorry. Is it wrong that I stopped caring?"

"We all had a lot going on," I continue. "I think what Merin needs most is a place to be safe."

"She has that right here with you. She can stay as long as she wants to."

"Thank you."

"You're welcome. It's really not a difficult thing to do."

Chapter Twenty-Nine

Merin

"*I'm sorry, Merin, but something has come to our attention...*"

My class organized a walk-out, but that didn't change the principal's mind. It didn't matter that I didn't sleep with Kelli. George's decision, however righteous and necessary, started an avalanche, and fleeing my home was all I could do not to be taken over by it.

Home.

There's nothing left for me there. Fiona still sends text messages. After another heated conversation with Ellen and my parents, I packed my bags and took a flight, then drove the rest of the way up here, and now...

I'm free. I'm scared. For the first time in my life, without the safety net that I thought my family and community would always provide in time of need—because I was always ready to do the same for them. I didn't realize it came with conditions.

I have kept my own room at the B&B. Kelli doesn't push.

Perhaps, sometimes, I wish that she would. We have breakfast together, spend the days visiting the surroundings, while I tell her of my last days home.

We never raise *that* question.

But we have dinner at her parents', two people who act like it's completely normal for a stranger to show up out of the blue and insert herself into their routines.

"I have to make a little trip tomorrow, for work," Kelli says. "You could come with me, but you'd have to spend a few hours by yourself."

"I believe Merin can do that," Maxine says, a tad amused. I know what she means, even though I'm grateful Kelli has been shielding me from everyone and everything these past days.

"If it's all the same to you, I'd like to stay here...take a walk, finish my book." The Jamesons keep a small library for their guests. Books have been a part of trying to delay the inevitable, figuring out what I'm going to do.

I don't assume there'd be many jobs for me around here.

"Of course." Everyone is so kind, so accommodating. Without conditions, as it seems, and still, there's something missing.

It's a miracle that I even notice when it's been missing from my life for so long.

We say goodbye after dinner as always, but something's different tonight. I think about what George said, his passionate plea for using the time we had.

He was right.

I feel like a teenager sneaking out of their parents' house, giddy, a tad guilty. But I'm not a teenager—I'm a grown woman whose marriage, and so much more, ended. Time to end the guilt too.

Kelli doesn't even look surprised when she opens the door to me. She just pulls me in and kisses me softly.

"Can I just stay with you? Like that other time?"

If she's disappointed with that, she doesn't let it show, but perhaps she hopes, like me, that we can go somewhere from here.

"You'll always have a place with me," she whispers, and it's only then I realize how much grieving I still have to do. But I found a safe place to do it.

Chapter Thirty

Kelli

"Glad to see you in one piece, Jameson."

"Thank you, sir. I'm sorry I couldn't find Lucas earlier." Here, in the context of work, I have to go that far at least. Even though doing my boss's friends a favor was part of my cover story, there's also part of it that was true.

I didn't want this assignment.

He thought it would help me "cool my heels" after I crossed a line with a suspect accused of murdering a woman and abducting another. I'm not sure that was what happened, but here I am back, kind of, in one piece. I must have done something right.

"About that...I'm going to need some time off. For personal reasons."

He looks surprised. "You've been away longer than planned as it is."

"Consulting in the corruption case...after Lucas Gavin turned up dead."

It's not something he can argue with.

"How long?"

"I don't know, another couple of weeks at least. I'll check in with you."

"I'd appreciate that," he mutters. "All right. Good job—and good on you for not going off on another suspect. Keep it that way."

"I plan to. Thanks. Sir," I acknowledge the somewhat back-handed compliment.

"Whatever it is you're going to do, I hope you can find some closure. You earned it."

Have I?

When I leave the office and get in my car to drive back, I think that the jury's still out on that. I'm going to make good use of the time.

I can't wait to go home to Merin, and for another night of holding her close to me, for the moment when this will be more for her than a last resort.

We still have a chance.

Chapter
Thirty-One

Merin

There's a reason why I chose to stay at the B&B rather than accompany Kelli to the city. The book...I'll admit that was an excuse though I enjoy reading the lesbian mystery, out in the open, in the armchair by the fireplace. It's getting chillier.

At some point, I won't be able to avoid trips to the city any longer, to look for work, but I'm content to take a day and fantasize about the possibilities.

Kelli has been so very patient with me—but I guess she's aware that I don't bring much with me other than fantasies, and the memory of that one time George and I agreed to never talk about again.

But now the sky is the limit. Kelli is figuring out her professional future, and so will I. Tonight, sleeping next to her might not be all I want to do.

Kelli is on her way back. I've gone to the small supermarket a ten-minute walk away from the B&B and snuck in a bottle of champagne. Damn right, we're alive, and after a tornado flattened your house and someone in your family almost went to prison...

There are many reasons to celebrate. I'm tired of waiting, and I'm sure she is too.

I'm taking Sam, who has taken a liking to me, out on a walk before Kelli returns.

It's a cloudy day, wind tearing at my clothes, though it's nothing like the day of the tornado. Some rain, and tides higher than usual, but we're not in any danger.

There was a time when I thought I could never live anywhere but what I considered home, the land, and the people...Apparently, I wasn't as tethered as I thought.

In the distance, someone is flying a kite. The image feels appropriate.

Flying.

High.

Scared, but free. The sky's the limit, even if it's cloudy and grey.

I become aware of Sam tugging at his leash. He's well behaved and knows the way home, but I still prefer the leash when I'm alone with him.

"That's not the way we're going, buddy," I tell him. "Come on, Kelli will be home soon."

I swear he perks up at hearing her name, but he still wants to go in the wrong direction, closer to the water where a small group of people has gathered. I know some of the guests who are staying at the Jamesons'—none of them are among them.

"Come on. Sam."

"I'm calling an ambulance," I hear someone say, and for a second or so, my grip on reality and Sam's leash weakens. I never saw Lucas Gavin's body, after he was shot, or when the police fished him out of the lake.

I don't want to be near any of this, but I'm drawn to the scene, nonetheless.

It's a young woman, sparsely dressed and barely conscious.

Spooked, I reel back. Sam, sensing my discomfort, keeps close now. In the distance, I hear sirens. There's nothing I can do here.

"Sam! Let's go!"

The sky opens at that moment, and we hurry back up the same path we came to get back into the shelter of the B&B.

The look on her face is still haunting me, and I know this story isn't over.

Epilogue: Before the Storm

Lexi

She couldn't believe it had worked, how stupid they were. Now that she, Amanda, and Fiona had publicly distanced themselves from Erica, not only did Lucas and his gang think they were easy prey, but they also thought the girls were on their side.

Lexi wasn't sure that they had an actual plan. They had rage to motivate them, and for starters, that was enough.

She made sure to keep her glass in sight at all times. Money really bought a lot of things. Lexi was sure the bartender knew that she was underage, but Lucas just flashed the false ID and his platinum credit card, and he kept the drinks coming.

Not this time. One click, two rings, and Fiona and Amanda would be there.

Okay, so they had somewhat of a plan.

And it worked like a charm.

Lucas was already more than blitzed.

"I'll be right back," he said, leaning in with that little condescending smile.

Lexi contained her impulse to throw up, and when he headed to the bathroom, she had his cell phone in her hands. The trial had come and gone quickly—too quickly. Had anyone even looked at his phone, his internet activities? Lexi had some skills, and it didn't take her long to unearth a few pictures and text messages.

We're golden, Kyle Vance had texted. *What's the next stage?*

The phone nearly dropped from her fingers when she saw the picture that Lucas had shared with him and Bradley.

How much ransom could we get?

You're sick man. Did your parents cut your allowance?

It's not about the money, Lucas answered. *It's about testing the limits.*

Like you did with Erica?

Now you're getting it.

Lucas returned soon after, oblivious to the fact that she had gone ghostly pale. He didn't notice it either when Lexi slipped the phone back into the pocket of his coat.

"Hey, how about we go somewhere less noisy?"

Hey, how about we kill you? She didn't say it out loud, instead enacted the secret signal.

"I'm really sorry, not tonight. A friend of mine has an emergency. I need to see her, now."

"Now? Come on. What if I had an emergency tonight?"

She all but jumped back.

"Sorry, Lucas. Good night. I'll see you."

She left the bar almost running.

Amanda was waiting for her in the parking lot.

Amanda

I t was when Lexi told her what she'd witnessed, in tears, that Amanda realized they were in over their heads. The truth about what Lucas did to Erica was horrible. They never thought he might want to go further than covering it up.

A freaking psychopath.

A psychopath with friends who understood him. Got his back.

Sharing pictures of Lexi's little sister and talking about kidnapping her.

"What if we went to the police?"

"Cross and LeBlanc?" Lexi shook her head. "They'll always side with them. I have no proof I saw those messages, and I'm sure Lucas will delete them."

"We could get his phone. You managed once. And this time we bring it to the police."

"I don't know. I don't trust them. We need to do something!"

"I agree. Look, Kyle and Pete are cowards. They'll do whatever Lucas says. If we could scare him..."

"With what?" Lexi asked, resigned. "His parents own the town. No. I'll have to talk to my parents. We need to move out of this freaking town."

"There might be something else we can do," Amanda said. "We don't have proof, how about we make him think we do? He trusts you, right?"

Lexi shrugged. "I guess."

"So, if you asked him to meet you, maybe even smoke some pot together, he'd come, right?"

"Let's go see Fiona," Amanda decided.

They drove to the Collins' house, where they found Fiona's mother sitting at the kitchen table with her sister, their history teacher Mrs. Burke.

Briefly, Amanda wondered if they'd notice that Lexi had cried—or that she'd had alcohol that night. Neither would be good.

"We're just here to see Fiona," she said. "I promise we won't stay long."

"She's upstairs," Mrs. Collins answered. "Would you like some tea?"

"No, thanks." She avoided Mrs. Burke's curious gaze, and she and Lexi went upstairs.

Fiona was sitting at her desk, swiveling the chair around when they came in.

"How did it go?" she asked.

"We need to do something," Lexi said.

"Lucas is even worse than we thought," Amanda added. "We need to do something, and quick. You still have that ammunition in your garage that no one remembers?"

Fiona gave her a quizzical look. "You want to shoot him?"

"I wish...But I think if we could just scare him a little, that would help."

"Sure." Fiona didn't sound sure at all. "That's ammunition. Anyone has access to a rifle that works with that?"

"I do," Lexi said.

They were all silent for a moment, all, Amanda assumed, thinking the same thing.

The day Lucas Gavin got scared would be a good day for all of them.

For the longest time he and his friends had gotten away with what everyone called "pranks." Then, there was Erica.

It had to stop somewhere.

Fiona

I t had to stop. This was the only way they could make it happen. Lucas's rage was so grotesque, at Erica, at all of them for daring to question him.

Fiona, on the other hand, was terrified. A twitch of the finger, a deafening sound, and he was clutching his chest, a look of disbelief on his face.

Someone had to stop him, she reminded herself.

"It was an accident," Lexi spoke in an urgent tone. "He was attacking you."

Yes, he was, but maybe they could have stopped him together?

"Think of what he did to Erica. What they were going to do. If Lucas is gone, the others will back down. It was an accident," Amanda repeated."

"Yes," Fiona said. "Yes, it was."

No one would ever find the gun. Or the body.

But Erica would be safe in all of this, because for all everyone knew, they hadn't spoken to her in weeks.

"It's over," she said, which was only a part of the truth, but the part that would carry them through what they'd have to do next. "Let's clean this up."

Fiona saw her grim determination reflected in her friends' faces.

She was still scared, but a little less so.

Acknowledgments

T hank you -

Dominique, for everything.

Lauren Eve, for allowing me to use your beautiful poetry in this book. These lines made me think of Kelli and Merin when I first saw them.

My readers who follow me to the sometimes darker places my mind goes. I promise that there's always a happy ending eventually!

About the Author

B arbara Winkes writes sapphic crime drama and Christmas romance. She loves writing characters who get the
job done, whether it's stopping a predator or saving cherished
traditions—while still making time for love. She lives with her
wife in Quebec City.

barbarawinkes.com

Also by Barbara Winkes

The Crossing Lines Trilogy
Undercover
Redemption
Vengeance

The Connected Series
Promised to the Queen
Drawn to the Enemy
Tempted by the Protector